solid start
ANNIE OPRAY

PENGUIN BOOKS

Penguin Books

Published by the Penguin Group
Penguin Books Australia Ltd
250 Camberwell Road
Camberwell, Victoria 3124, Australia
Penguin Books Ltd
80 Strand, London WC2R 0RL, England
Penguin Putnam Inc.
375 Hudson Street, New York, New York 10014, USA
Penguin Books, a division of Pearson Canada
10 Alcorn Avenue, Toronto, Ontario, Canada, M4V 3B2
Penguin Books (NZ) Ltd
Cnr Rosedale and Airborne Roads, Albany, Auckland, New Zealand
Penguin Books (South Africa) (Pty) Ltd
24 Sturdee Avenue, Rosebank, Johannesburg 2196, South Africa
Penguin Books India (P) Ltd
11, Community Centre, Panchsheel Park, New Delhi 110 017, India

First published by Penguin Books Australia 2003

1 3 5 7 9 10 8 6 4 2

Designed by Melissa Fraser, Penguin Design Studio
Typeset in 10/14 pt Helvetica Light by Post Pre-press Group,
Brisbane, Queensland
Printed and bound in Australia by McPherson's Printing Group,
Maryborough, Victoria

National Library of Australia
Cataloguing-in-Publication data:

Opray, Annie, 1961– .
Solid start: advice and recipes for starting your baby on solids.

Includes index.
ISBN 0 14 300059 4.

1. Baby foods. 2. Infants – Nutrition. 3. Cookery (Baby foods). I. Title.

641.5622

www.penguin.com.au

Penguin Books

solid start

Annie Opray is a chef who specialises in food for babies and toddlers.

She initially worked in marketing before deciding to obtain a cooking qualification. The combination of these experiences led her and her husband, Christopher, to successfully establish a restaurant, function centre and bed and breakfast in country Victoria.

Destiny called after the birth of her daughter, however, as Annie soon discovered there was a need to help new parents with the sometimes daunting task of introducing solid food to their babies. Her business 'Solid Start' was born.

Annie's classes cover theory, nutritional information and cooking demonstrations of recipes suitable for babies and toddlers. Annie and her business have been featured in newspapers and Annie has appeared regularly on television. This book is the result of the numerous questions that she has been asked along the way.

195 795

To Christopher and to Lexie,
who proves the most wonderful things are possible.

ACKNOWLEDGEMENTS

I would like to thank my daughter, Lexie, for being a very special little sous chef, for her patience and for all the fun we had preparing the recipes.

Thanks also to my tasting team: Hannah, Tilly and James.

My thanks to Kay Gibbons, Manager of Nutrition Services at The Royal Children's Hospital, Melbourne, for reviewing the manuscript and providing invaluable advice and assistance.

My appreciation also goes to my editor, Susan McLeish, for her skill and professionalism.

Finally, to Christopher and my family and friends, a big thank you because your interest and encouragement made this book so much easier to write.

FOREWORD

The introduction of your baby's first solids should be a very exciting time in their development. However, sometimes the pleasure of seeing your baby move to this exciting milestone can be overshadowed by anxiety or concern about exactly what to do or how to do it.

In this little book, and in the cooking classes she offers, Annie Opray provides practical tips and information to help you feel confident about preparing your baby's food, including what to offer, when and how much. Fresh foods are the ideal basis of first solids, and Annie shows how to make sure meals using these are enjoyable and of maximum benefit.

Increasingly, research allows us to understand more about the importance of early nutrition on long-term health. This information often causes many parents to worry a great deal about their children's eating. However, we also understand that trying 'too hard' to ensure children eat well is likely to be counter productive. Children are much more likely to eat well, and to develop life-long good eating practices, if they see their parents eating and enjoying a range of healthy foods.

Eating is obviously important for growth and development, but it is also a time for great enjoyment and social interaction. Fostering the pleasure associated with eating, and making sure that mealtimes are relaxed and social, is an essential part of healthy eating. Feeling confident about feeding your child can make this easier.

Kay Gibbons
Manager of Nutrition Services at
The Royal Children's Hospital, Melbourne
February 2003

CONTENTS

INTRODUCTION

In my experience there is nothing more wonderful than being a parent. However, it must be said that along with the highest of the highs come some lows. Often you can wish your baby came with an instruction manual, and it's reassuring to find that lots of other parents, especially first-timers, feel the same way.

Through my business, Solid Start, I have been helping parents understand the nutritional needs of their baby and how to meet those needs. Over numerous cooking classes and information sessions I have heard lots of questions from parents – some obvious, some a bit more obscure, but none of them irrelevant. Starting your baby on solid food might sound simple for those who haven't tried it, but often it is one of the biggest challenges for parents. *Solid Start* is designed to help make the process easier by answering some of these questions.

Part 1 begins by discussing good nutrition, a healthy diet in general and the particular dietary requirements of babies. It then moves on to the business of actually introducing those foods to your baby and offers practical advice and tips, such as when to start, what the first food should be, and how to deal with a fussy eater.

Part 2 offers over 90 recipes to help you tempt your little one onto delicious and nutritious solid food. Each recipe has been developed with a baby's nutritional needs in mind and they are presented in age groups: 4–6 months, 6–9 months, 9–12 months, and one year plus. This organisation is both for easy reference and to allow you to be confident that you are giving your baby the right foods at the right time, from the moment they try their first rice cereal to their first family meal as a toddler.

Practicality has also played a major role in the formulation of the recipes; most of them use ingredients that are readily available, if not already in your pantry, and they do not take long to prepare, which is important in a busy day. Even better news is that with a few enhancements, many of the recipes can be converted to family meals for those times you can all sit down together.

I hope you enjoy *Solid Start* and that it makes your life as a parent just a little easier.

GETTING STARTED

WHY IS SOLID FOOD REQUIRED?

At first it is hard to believe that all your newborn needs to thrive is milk, but this becomes obvious when you find yourself buying larger and larger sizes of baby clothes! Soon the time comes, however, when milk alone is not enough to meet their growing needs and solid food becomes a must.

This is usually between four and six months of age. After six months a baby's iron stores are very low and they need solid food to prevent iron deficiency. Babies of this age also require the other nutritional building blocks found in food, such as vitamins, minerals and protein, to ensure that they continue to develop at the appropriate rate.

Offering sold food also encourages the development of fine motor skills, particularly when babies begin to feed themselves.

physical benefits

A balanced diet is essential for your baby's overall general physical wellbeing and is the cornerstone of a healthy lifestyle. Good eating practices should be established early to ensure a healthy growth rate and sufficient energy levels. A healthy diet aids in the development of the brain, bones, teeth and organs, and helps your body to function at the optimum level (see Chapter 3 for more information).

The action of eating solid food also has physical benefits. It helps babies develop an efficient chewing action, strengthens muscles and helps with jaw development. The finger food stage, at around nine months of age, promotes hand–eye coordination.

social skills and independence

Even in the early stages, the inclusion of food in a baby's diet teaches them social skills that are part of our everyday lives – although it may take them a while to master the manners that go along with it.

The way babies are taught to eat in the early stages affects their future patterns. When babies are as young as six months of age it is important they have mealtimes in their highchair as this teaches them it is not acceptable to run around and eat food, which can be dangerous.

The journey of babies in their first year of life from total dependence to the beginning of independence is a natural pro-gression and fascinating to watch. One example of this is the feeding process.

At the beginning it is the parent who is in charge at meal-times but as the months pass and the baby becomes more proficient at eating they naturally wish to play a larger part. Some parents want to prolong the initial stage, when they are in charge of the spoon, but eventually the baby will want to feed themselves. This is when the fun really begins!

question Kathy asks: 'My baby, Sam, is seven months old and he just adores his milk. I've tried and tried but he shows very little interest in food and I was wondering if I can delay solids until later?'

answer Some babies take longer to develop an appetite for solid food, but after six months milk alone will not meet all their nutritional requirements. Persevere in serving Sam a healthy mixture of solid foods and be patient, because the closer he gets to twelve months the more his appetite will swing in favour of food.

2

WHEN SHOULD I INTRODUCE SOLID FOOD?

When you first arrive home with your newborn baby, the days and nights are consumed with frequent breast or bottle feeds, coping with the lack of sleep and trying to establish that elusive routine that others seem to talk about so easily.

Any consideration of solid food seems a long way off, but then the months skip past and suddenly your baby starts showing signs they're ready to be introduced to the wonderful world of food.

How do you know when your baby is really ready? If you are not sure but think your baby may be ready, there is nothing to lose by trying: you can always stop and re-try in a few weeks. Having said that, and although a lot of first-time parents are keen to reach this milestone, there is no need to rush into it as your baby will be eating for the next eighty years or so. While it is by no means an exact science, there are some reliable indicators that will help you to determine the right time.

age

Solid food is usually introduced to babies of four to six months of age. Earlier introduction can harm the digestive system and create problems with food allergies, and some experts recommend commencing solids closer to six months. The timing will vary depending on the baby. In the case of a very premature baby, it may be later because their actual age is impacted by how early they were delivered. In most of these situations the baby will be under the care of a paediatrician who will be in the best position to advise about solid food.

curiosity

A sign your baby may be ready for solid food is when they start demonstrating great curiosity in others' eating habits. They may mimic you, taking their hand to their mouth, or may pay a lot of attention to what's on your plate! Often it is an outsider's observation that alerts new parents to this curiosity and this, combined with other indicators, makes them realise their baby is ready for solid food.

everything in the mouth

When your baby starts putting everything in their mouth, such as toys, their fist or your fingers, they may be telling you they are ready for solid food. This behaviour can also be related to teething but for most babies it is a reliable indicator that they are ready for food, especially in the early stages.

grizzly patch

Babies who are usually contented may develop a 'grizzly' patch at a particular time each day. This occurs when they are actually beginning to become hungry for solid food. You will know this is the case if it happens repeatedly. Bear in mind that it may not necessarily be at breakfast, lunch or dinnertime, as babies have no concept of our eating routines. It may be at 10.00 in the morning or 2.30 in the afternoon and will vary depending on the baby.

slow weight gain

Sometimes the introduction of solid food is recommended if your baby has slow or no weight gain and this will be closely monitored through your health centre. There the potential solutions should be discussed with health professionals to ensure the best course of action for you and your baby.

question Sally asks: 'My friend told me to start Joseph on solids at three months because it would help him sleep through the night. Is this the right thing to do?'

answer If this theory was correct, most sleep-deprived mothers would be thrilled. Unfortunately it is not. In fact, starting solids too early is not recommended as it can harm your baby's digestive system and create problems with food allergies. At three months all Joseph needs to thrive is breast milk or formula. Wait until he shows signs of being ready to start on solid food, which may not happen until around six months of age, and will definitely not be before four months.

WHAT SOLID FOODS ARE REQUIRED?

Not unlike an adult's diet, your baby's diet should consist of lots of breads, cereals, fruit and vegetables, a moderate amount of lean red meat, pork, poultry, fish, eggs, milk, cheese and yoghurt, and only small amounts of butter, margarine, oils and sugar. Babies also have special requirements with regard to full-fat, low-salt and low-sugar products. It is important that you are aware of these and the essential nutrients so that you can select the right types of foods for your baby.

fresh is best

Fresh ingredients and produce should feature in the food you prepare for your baby as they provide maximum nutritional value and flavour. Processed and canned foods should be considered as a secondary option and only used occasionally. While processed baby foods will not harm your baby there are some very strong reasons why they should not form the foundation of your baby's diet.

Most processed foods have a smoother texture than food

you prepare at home and therefore do not encourage your baby to progress to more textured food at the recommended rate.

Some products include items such as modified maize starch, a thickening agent. These ingredients bulk up the content of the food without adding any nutritional value. Some products also have a high salt content, which is not good for your baby's small kidneys.

There will definitely be days when you need to rely on processed foods, but you should compare the labels and provide the best of what is available (see Chapter 8 for more information).

full-fat

Babies must have a *full-fat* diet to continue to grow and develop at an appropriate rate. It is very important that your baby's diet does not include any low-fat products. However, your baby's diet should not include large amounts of butter or oil as too much fat is not good for them either. A good example of the low-fat versus full-fat approach is cow's milk. Cow's milk will be your baby's main source of milk once your child is 12 months old and after you stop breastfeeding. If you purchase a low-fat milk for yourself you will also need to buy a full-cream milk for your baby.

low-salt

If you try to imagine the size of your baby's kidneys, it is not surprising to realise that they are not able to process much sodium chloride, commonly known as salt. Although babies need an appropriate amount of salt in their diet this can be derived naturally from fresh produce. Many processed products are already high in salt, even before seasoning is added at home during or after cooking, so be careful when shopping. Wherever possible you should select low-salt alternatives, such as butter and margarine, stocks, canned tomatoes and tomato paste. Many new parents say this approach assists them in reducing the amount of salt in their own diets as well. Aside from potential kidney damage, too much salt can help produce a fussy eater because your baby will become thirsty and consume more liquid, leaving little room for food.

low-sugar

Due primarily to concerns relating to tooth decay, it is recommended you minimise your baby's intake of refined sugar. Sugar, sweet biscuits and jam are just a few examples of products high in refined sugar. We do, however, live in the real world and treats can be enjoyed occasionally. Again, look for low-sugar alternatives, such as jam made with 100 per cent fruit.

carbohydrates

Carbohydrates provide an excellent source of energy, which is particularly important for babies as they grow and are able to do increasingly physical things, such as roll over, crawl and walk.

Complex carbohydrates, which come from foods such as cereal, pasta, potatoes, bread, rice, noodles, baked beans, grains and fruit (particularly bananas), are good for your baby and should be encouraged. Sugar also belongs in the carbohydrate family and there are two types. The first is naturally occurring sugar, which can be found in fruits such as grapes, apples, oranges, apricots and sultanas. This sugar is good for your baby and such produce is an integral part of a healthy diet. The second sugar group is referred to as refined sugar and should be avoided as much as possible (see page 12).

vitamins

Vitamins are not produced naturally by the body and therefore must be ingested. We are fortunate to have an excellent selection of fruit and vegetables in Australia, which enables you to provide ample amounts of vitamins in your baby's daily diet. Unless medically recommended, it should not be necessary for you to provide your baby with vitamin supplements.

It is important to be aware of the main vitamin groups and their physiological benefits.

- Vitamin A, found in foods such as dairy foods, eggs, fish and lettuce, helps to develop good eyesight, healthy skin tissue and tooth enamel.
- Vitamin B is important as it assists with the function of the nervous system and the formation of red blood cells, and also helps to release the energy contained within other

food groups such as proteins, fats and carbohydrates. Foods rich in vitamin B include leafy vegetables, bread, meat, fish and brown rice.

- Vitamin C, found in many fruits and vegetables, such as oranges and potatoes, and parsley, is required for healthy gums, teeth and blood vessels as well as assisting with the absorption of iron.
- Vitamin D works with calcium and phosphorous for strong bone development, which is of particular importance for babies, whose bones are growing at a rapid rate. Dairy foods such as butter, margarine, milk and cheese are a good source of vitamin D.

minerals

Minerals are necessary in your baby's diet to promote healthy blood, strong bones and growth. The two minerals that are particularly essential are iron and calcium.

Babies have very high iron needs because they grow so fast. Sufficient iron levels help to ensure healthy blood and muscles. Most babies are born with a store of iron that becomes depleted at around six months of age. You will find many products for babies of this age, such as rice cereal and formula, are iron-enriched. Other foods that will deliver good levels of iron are red meat, liver, kidneys, poultry, fish, beans, green leafy vegetables, wheatgerm and wholegrain cereals. A healthy intake of foods rich in vitamin C ensures iron is absorbed well.

Calcium is very important for healthy bones and teeth. Between 70 and 75 per cent of calcium intake comes from milk and other dairy products, such as yoghurt and cheese.

protein

Protein is an essential part of your baby's diet because it provides energy, assists with growth and helps with the repair and maintenance of tissue, including muscle.

There are two important protein groups: 'animal' and 'plant'. Animal proteins come from foods such as chicken, fish, egg white, meat, dairy products and offal. Plant proteins come from rice, cereals, wheatgerm, pasta, lentils, bread and flour.

It is important you select from both food groups to provide your baby with the proper balance of protein that ensures they have plenty of energy to do all the things that babies enjoy doing.

water

Water is required to maintain adequate hydration.

In the days prior to commencing solid foods, babies receive sufficient water through breast milk or formula. Once they advance to solid food, water is provided in purees, which usually have a high liquid content. It is important to include the cooking liquid in a puree as it contains many of the nutrients of the fruit or vegetable being served.

Once your baby is eating more textured food, you should be

offering them water a few times a day, particularly in warmer weather. Some parents express concern that their baby may drink too much water, which will leave little room for food. However, most babies tend to drink water only to quench their thirst (rather than for the sweetness, which is more the case with juice). It is common practice to give your baby cooled, boiled (that is, sterilised) water in the beginning but this need not continue after six months. Water also helps to clean your baby's teeth before they can do so properly with a toothbrush.

question Janet asks: 'I try to be good and watch my weight so I buy low-fat milk and yoghurt. Are they okay to give my ten-month-old baby Daniel?'

answer Low-fat products may work for you, but they are not appropriate for babies and toddlers. Daniel needs a full-fat diet to provide the concentrated nutrients to enable him to have the energy to achieve the important milestones.

HOW TO INTRODUCE SOLID FOOD

Once you have decided the time has come to introduce solid food, there are some guidelines that may make the transition from a milk-only diet a little easier for both you and your baby.

choose the best time

Many people consider mid-morning a good time to first try solid food, but because babies are all different it is better to try at the time when your baby is at their happiest and most relaxed. Once again, it is important to keep in mind that your baby does not conform to adult mealtimes and, as you may have already discovered, they can be a law unto themselves.

liquid or solids first?

When your baby first starts on solid food and for some months thereafter it is appropriate to offer milk before food, with sufficient periods of time in between. However, as they become more used to solid food and their appetite develops you can switch to serving the food first and the milk afterwards (see the Daily Menu Guide on page 57).

the first food

Often rice cereal is the first food offered to babies as it is easily digestible and has good levels of iron and calcium. Furthermore, it is specially formulated for infants and is less allergenic than other cereals. It is important you wash your hands thoroughly before preparing the cereal and that you use clean and dry utensils.

To begin with it is recommended you mix one part cereal to two parts liquid and stir until you achieve a smooth texture. If the mixture is too thick, adjust the consistency by adding more liquid. The liquid can be either breast milk, formula or cooled boiled water. It is very difficult to recommend an average quantity as each baby's needs are different. However, as a general guideline, one teaspoon of rice cereal to two teaspoons of liquid is a good starting point. Once your baby masters the physical action of eating, the teaspoon quantity will become a tablespoon and then two tablespoons. For babies over six months old, three tablespoons of cereal to six tablespoons of liquid would be appropriate. Rice cereal can also be used as a base as many things can be added to it to enhance the flavour and texture, such as pureed fruit and vegetables.

new foods in isolation

In order to be sure your baby is not allergic to certain foods, it is suggested that each new food is introduced into your baby's diet separately and monitored.

While the chances of an allergic reaction are relatively low, special care must be taken as babies' immune systems are immature and still developing. There are certain foods that are more prone to generate a reaction, such as eggs (especially the white), fish, peanut products, strawberries, honey and cow's milk, and these need to be introduced into your baby's diet at particular stages of their development (see Chapter 7 for more information).

Another school of thought suggests that some foods, such as water-based vegetables like zucchini or golden squash, are unlikely to cause a reaction and can therefore be tried mixed with other foods. In terms of practicality and to ensure your baby enjoys the widest range of tastes and textures available, this may be worth considering.

second and third meals

After your baby is happily eating solid food once a day, which may take some time, introduce a second meal and then a month or so later a third meal.

The pattern of introduction will vary. I have met some babies who fall in love with solid food from the very beginning and, conversely, I have consoled the parents of babies who at 10 months seem totally disinterested in food. In these cases the babies seem to prefer milk over food but eventually the balance does swing in favour of food. It is important to remember that food is a complement to milk and not a replacement, especially in the first 12 months. As your baby's reliance on solid food increases, their average daily milk intake decreases from approximately 900 ml at four months to around 600 ml after 12 months (see the Daily Menu Guide on page 57).

quantity

Quantity depends on the individual – it is not a good idea to compare how much your baby is eating with how much other babies are eating. Begin by offering one teaspoon and gradually increase the quantity over a few days until your baby is having one or two tablespoons at a time. The quantity will increase further over time, but at a different rate for each baby.

Between six and nine months most babies are enjoying three meals, one snack and three to four milk feeds a day. During this time, the morning milk feed may be dropped as your baby's reliance on solid food increases. A good indicator for this is if you consistently find yourself tipping half the bottle down the sink – obviously it is a little more difficult to judge when you are breast feeding. Between the ages of nine and twelve months most babies will be having three meals a day with three milk feeds.

Remember, as long as your baby is gaining weight and has a happy disposition you can safely assume they are having a sufficient amount of food.

texture

The challenge of texture is often mentioned by parents as a major concern.

On the one hand many parents are told that at particular points in time their babies should be at certain stages: beginning with purees or smooth mashes, progressing to fork mashes by nine months of age, then large, diced finger food as they approach 12 months, and finally, after the age of one, babies should be having chewy, finger and family-type food. However, as with other growth and development, such as crawling, walking and talking, every baby is different and will reach these milestones when they are good and ready. As the baby's parent you know best when your child is ready to move on to the next stage. At this point introduce them to foods at the next level but if your baby is constantly gagging and mealtimes have become an unhappy event for both of you, revert to the previous stage and try to move on again in a couple of weeks. As long as your baby is not lagging more than a few months behind the guidelines there is no need to worry.

Many parents equate their baby's having teeth with their ability to tackle more textured food, but most babies will have mastered the scissor-like action required to chew fairly early on, teeth or no teeth. So try not to let a lack of teeth discourage you from introducing more textured food.

supervision

It is of the utmost importance that you supervise your baby whenever they are eating. It just takes a moment for food to lodge in a baby's throat, sometimes with disastrous and tragic consequences. You and your partner should be familiar with how to deal with an emergency. Most parents have a story to tell about an incident involving gagging or choking but learning what to do in such situations will make you feel more confident as you introduce your child to solids.

For the same reason, it is vital you do not allow your baby to walk or run around while eating food. When at home, your baby should, from a very young age, have all meals in their highchair. In fact, the highchair should be your baby's special place and one they actually enjoy being in at mealtimes.

taste everything

You need to be very sure about the temperature and texture of all the food you give to your baby and a good way to do this is to taste everything, but with a separate spoon. Some parents are surprised that they should use a separate spoon, but doing so minimises the chance of passing on infections, such as cold or flu, through saliva. Your baby's immune system takes time to develop. This means they are vulnerable to many germs and viruses that may not be as serious in adults.

Tasting the food allows you to be confident that it is not too hot, as most babies prefer their food at room temperature or just warm.

If you are tasting for flavour, however, bear in mind that a baby's tastebuds react to flavours at many times the strength of an adult's, so what may seem bland to you will taste quite different to your baby. Conversely, if something tastes sweet, salty or spicy to you, it will taste even stronger to your child.

question Robyn asks: 'I am worried about my little girl Sophie who will still only eat pureed food and she is nine months old. A friend from playgroup said her little boy is already having lumpy food and that I should make Sophie have that too. Is this the right approach?'

answer It is always a source of worry to compare one baby to another because they never progress at the same rate. Firstly, you should never force your baby to do anything and this certainly applies in the case of food. If Sophie is constantly gagging on lumpy food she is not physically ready to move on from purees. Give her a bit more time, then try mixing just a few lumps in with her pureed food. Continue with this approach for a few days then slowly thicken the texture. This gradual approach should ensure mealtimes remain pleasant for both you and Sophie.

5

HELPFUL TIPS

In days gone by, it was often commonplace to have your own parents and possibly other relatives pass on their experience and advice firsthand. But times change, and because you may not necessarily have that luxury these tips may prove helpful.

tooth decay

We all know that sweet substances can lead to tooth decay and therefore should be avoided. But fewer people realise that leaving a bottle of milk in your baby's mouth while they are sleeping can also result in damage to teeth and gums. When we sleep we do not secrete much saliva, which contains an agent that counteracts the sucrose in sugar. Therefore, it is important that if your baby takes a bottle of milk to bed, you remove it as soon as it is finished. Better still, get into the practice of having milk prior to bedtime, which will avoid the problem altogether.

cow's milk

Cow's milk alone does not have the right composition of nutrients and minerals to allow babies under 12 months to thrive, hence the need for breastmilk and formula. Breastfeeding is encouraged even beyond 12 months but many mothers switch their babies to cow's milk at this time.

To introduce cow's milk into your baby's diet, adopt a gradual approach by combining it with your baby's regular type of milk for a few days.

It is interesting to note that cow's milk can be used in small amounts in cooking from when your baby reaches six months. Once again, a gradual introduction is recommended and a good way to begin is by using it on your baby's rice cereal, initially blending it with their regular liquid, whether that be breastmilk, formula or cooled boiled water. Over the course of a few days swing the balance to cow's milk, which should start to make your life a little easier. You will then be able to use cow's milk in other recipes, such as for a mornay sauce or a baked custard.

meat

Generally speaking, meat, poultry and fish can be included in your baby's diet from the age of six to eight months. These types of food are very high in essential nutrients such as iron, which is particularly important as your baby's iron stores need topping up after the first six months.

Many parents who have tried unsuccessfully to introduce meat into their baby's diet tell me their baby does not like the taste. It is unlikely that at the age of eight months their child has decided to become vegetarian, so it is more likely an issue of texture.

It is sometimes difficult to imagine your baby chewing through a piece of red meat, but selecting an appropriate method of cooking often helps a baby enjoy these types of food. Poaching is particularly suitable for baby food because it is a gentle method of cooking that results in a very soft structure. To poach meat, simply place it in a saucepan, cover with water and gently simmer with the lid on until it is cooked through. Retain the liquid for use in soups or sauces as it has a good nutritional value and plenty of flavour.

It is extremely important to ensure that the meat you give to your baby is well done as the cooking process destroys any bacteria that may be present in the food. At six to eight months of age most babies are still eating purees or fork-mashed food, and if this is the case you will need to puree or mash their meat as well. Include plenty of sauce with the meat as this will help your baby to swallow and digest it. It is sometimes difficult to achieve a good texture if you are blending a small amount of meat in a regular-sized blender and you may wish to try using a smaller appliance, such as a hand-held blender or a coffee grinder, for the initial very smooth purees.

eggs

One of the most-asked questions by parents is when to introduce egg into their baby's diet.

If your baby has other food allergies or a family history of primary eczema, asthma or hay fever, delaying the introduction of egg will give them time to develop a higher tolerance to the allergen. (See Chapter 7 for more information.)

In the absence of allergies, egg yolk can be tried when your baby is six months of age and the egg white tried between nine and twelve months. The egg white is introduced later as it is more likely to cause a reaction.

When introducing egg for the very first time, include a small amount (approximately half a teaspoon) of hard-boiled yolk in your baby's vegetables. When the time has come to try egg white, offer your baby a very small amount of scrambled egg. Once you know your baby is fine with egg you will be able to expand their menu considerably as many recipes feature egg as a binding ingredient.

herbs and spices

When cooking for your baby it is wise to avoid using very strong aromatic herbs and spices, such as chilli, garlic and curry. Sometimes, however, a baby may have a higher tolerance to stronger herbs and spices when their breastfeeding mother has eaten curries, for example, as a regular part of her diet. Milder herbs, such as parsley and basil, should not upset your baby's digestive system and when you are cooking a dish for the family to share often you can add these flavoursome herbs to enhance the taste.

parcooking

There are certain foods that while good for your baby are quite hard and if served uncooked can present a choking hazard. Examples of this include carrot, celery and apple. In the beginning, a good way to prepare these foods for your baby is to parcook them. This means peeling them, cutting them into fingers or other shapes and then cooking them for a short time until they are al dente. It is important to peel celery carefully as the string can be a challenge for a young eater. You should taste parcooked food before feeding it to your baby to be sure it is tender enough. Remember though, close supervision is always required at your baby's mealtimes.

Most babies like these foods cold from the fridge, especially in summer or when they are teething. Another good way of presenting harder fruit and vegetables to young babies is to grate them. Grating these foods can help minimise the risk of choking and, once babies are at the finger food stage, it can also provide good amusement value as they 'play' with the food on their highchair tray.

high-risk foods

Certain foods pose a higher risk of food poisoning because of their composition, including meat, poultry, eggs and fish. If these foods are not cooked to the right temperature or handled and stored correctly they can pose a major health threat, especially for a baby. Well-done meat is recommended for babies as bacteria is killed at over 65 degrees. Eliminating the conditions for bacteria to reproduce is vital and therefore storage in the refrigerator is appropriate as bacteria cannot grow below 4 degrees.

Honey is considered another high-risk food, due to its chemical composition and parents are recommended to delay the introduction of honey until after their baby has at least turned one and their immune system has further developed.

freezing

Fresh is undoubtedly best, but we live in a busy world and sometimes, despite the best efforts, it is not always achievable. When you are preparing food it is wise to cook large quantities and freeze some for later use. While a marginal amount of nutritional value will be lost by freezing, it is a much preferred option to processed baby food.

It is important that food be stored properly to avoid any bacterial contamination. Bacteria needs time, warmth and moisture to reproduce so these conditions must be eliminated. For example, cooked food should not be left on the bench until it is completely cold. As soon as it has cooled sufficiently it should be placed in the refrigerator or freezer. Many parents use ice-cube trays to freeze their baby's food. If you do use an ice-cube tray to store food in the freezer, it is preferable to use a covered tray to keep the food in the best condition possible. The ideal method of defrosting is to remove the food from the freezer and place it in the refrigerator 24 hours prior to use. If you find it hard to plan ahead, the next best option is to defrost using a microwave oven.

microwave

Given the busy life most parents lead, using the microwave may enable you to prepare something you may not otherwise have the time to do. It is important to remember that the microwave does not distribute heat evenly and therefore you must stir the heated food well to prevent any hot spots. As advised previously, you need to taste all food before giving it to your baby and in this case it is really the only way to be sure the food is the right temperature. Remember to taste with a separate spoon to avoid the transfer of bacteria from you to your baby.

leftovers

One of the most common errors in judgement made by new parents is to serve too much food. This is completely understandable, especially if you have taken hours to prepare a scrumptious meal for your baby. Alternatively, sometimes they are just not in the mood for what you are serving and after just one spoonful they opt for banana and yoghurt. In both cases this leaves a full plate that cannot be reused as it has been in contact with the baby's mouth and saliva and is therefore a potential breeding ground for bacteria. So it either goes in the bin or to the dog or cat, or it may even become a snack for you, which most parents will agree is not the best habit to develop. Try serving a small portion first, following it with a second helping if you meet with success.

suitable drinks

After the vital milk component of their daily diet has been consumed, water is by far the best liquid for your baby. Lead by example – babies love to imitate and will happily do so if they see you regularly enjoying water.

It is important not to offer your baby fizzy drinks, which are usually high in sugar. Some of these drinks also contain caffeine and, like tea and coffee, they are not suitable as they will overstimulate your baby. Similarly, some fruit juices contain sugar and they are not recommended for young babies, who are better off eating the whole fruit, which will provide some fibre as well.

question Christine asks: 'The other day I made a shepherd's pie and served a large helping to my baby Michael. He only had two mouthfuls and then decided he didn't want anymore. Is it okay to keep what he didn't eat and serve it for his lunch tomorrow?'

answer The shepherd's pie leftovers cannot be kept and served the next day as the meal has come into contact with Michael's saliva. This means there is a possibility of bacteria developing, which could lead to food poisoning. Try serving smaller portions with a second helping if required, to minimise wastage.

FUSSY EATERS

There are many challenges in raising a child and most parents would list fussy eating right up there in the top ten.

The majority of babies go through a fussy eating stage at around 14 months of age but the point to note here is that it *is* just a stage. An interesting statistic is that the average weight gain in a baby's first year is seven kilograms and in their second year it is only two – not much over a 12 month period. Therefore, assuming your baby is doing well in the health-centre check-ups and you continue to provide nutritious meals, you can rest assured that your baby is receiving sufficient food.

During a fussy eating stage, however, it can seem as though it may never end and the worry associated with it can cause much frustration and concern. If you are the parent of a fussy eater it is important you have as many strategies at your disposal as possible to help you through this difficult time.

small portions

It is often hard to comprehend how a fussy eater can continue to have the energy to play and run around when they nibble at their food. If they are playing and running happily, relax – they must be getting enough! Some toddlers simply don't need as much as others. If you're worried about food being left on the plate, consider serving a smaller portion and when it is gone giving a second helping if required. Remember that the quantity of food you serve to your baby or toddler should be relative to their size.

routine

As in most areas of their life, babies and toddlers appreciate routine at mealtimes. Perhaps your baby has become a fussy eater because their routine has changed significantly and they prefer the way it was. If possible revert to the previous routine, but if this is not practical be patient and give your baby some time to adjust to the new way of doing things.

texture

One of the most common reasons for a child becoming a fussy eater is that they are rebelling against an advance in the texture of their food for which they are not ready. While you should introduce your child to textured food in stages, it is wise to remember each baby will move at their own pace. If you suspect texture may be the reason for your baby becoming a fussy eater, take them back a stage and try to move them on again in a couple of weeks. Hopefully they will be ready then and will become their old self at mealtimes – happy and not frustrated.

too many snacks

At around the age of nine months your baby will start to become interested in finger food, and will begin to snack in between meals. At first you may wonder if there are enough hours in the day for snacks considering everything else they are doing, but somehow they fit it in. It is important to provide a selection of healthy snacks throughout the day to maintain their energy levels. However, there is a danger, particularly if you do not keep track, that your baby will oversnack and therefore have no room left at mealtimes for the food they need to thrive and grow. This often seems to be the case when you are out for the day, so remember to monitor your baby's intake of snacks to prevent fussy eating patterns.

too much fluid

Too much salted food will result in your baby consuming large amounts of fluid to quench their thirst. When this happens their stomach will be filled up with liquid leaving little or no room for nutritious food.

hungriest time

Many babies are actually hungriest early afternoon, so if practical serve the main meal at this time. This allows you to serve a light dinner such as fruit and yoghurt, which is easy to digest and less of a challenge for a tired baby. Parents sometimes question whether this approach will lead to hunger cries from their baby at 3.00 a.m., but it is the intake of food throughout the entire day, as opposed to just at dinnertime, that is important.

eliminate distractions

Sometimes after a busy day your baby may be tired, which makes them less likely to have a good meal. In this case they may need a little extra help. Try to create a relaxed and peaceful environment, keeping noise and other distractions to a minimum as much as possible. Take the time to sit with your baby and help them with eating. Talk to them about your day as this takes the focus off the food, allowing you to keep up a steady stream of spoonfuls, hopefully nearly unnoticed. Some parents of young fussy eaters say sitting their child in front of a video works well, but you need to consider the precedent you are setting for the future. Your baby will quickly come to expect this as their routine and it can be a very hard habit to break.

genuine dislikes

Genuine dislike of certain foods can be present early and if there are many foods in this group you will find yourself contending with a fussy eater. It is important to be patient, however, because studies have shown that you may sometimes need to try a new food between eight and ten times before your baby will accept it. This obviously takes time but it is worth doing because it minimises the chance of them becoming a fussy eater. If, on the other hand, you have persevered with the introduction of a particular food and your baby still does not accept it, recognise that it is probably a genuine dislike and move on.

power play

Some babies, particularly as they get older, come to realise that by refusing food they can assert their small but very effective power. They will continue to do this if they know they can make you react strongly to their actions. Therefore, your best response is to remain calm even though at times this may be a major challenge. If you can adopt this tactic your baby will soon lose interest in refusing food and mealtimes will become more peaceful.

don't try too long in the one sitting

It is often tempting to persevere with trying to cajole a fussy eater into eating, but this can go on far too long. The chances of a fussy eater accepting food diminish over time. Therefore, try your best but if the baby will still not eat after a reasonable time (15 to 20 minutes) remove the food and try again later.

encourage, don't stress

If you can encourage rather than criticise a fussy eater you are much more likely to get favourable results. However, this is definitely easier said than done, and most parents find it very difficult not to get stressed when their baby refuses to eat lovingly prepared food. When this is combined with worrying whether your baby is eating enough it can stretch even the most patient parent to their limit. Despite this it is important you do not get stressed or angry in this situation as it will make your baby less likely to eat. Another result of you losing your patience is that your baby may decide they do not like their highchair any more: they may associate you being cross with the highchair rather than their behaviour. If a fussy eater is getting you down, walk away for a moment, calm down and return to try again.

fresh air and exercise

Not unlike an adult's appetite, a baby's appetite can be stimulated by fresh air and exercise. It is important to include plenty of outdoor activities in your day, weather permitting, and to ensure your baby's activity levels are appropriate for their age group. The added bonus from this is that it should encourage a good night's sleep, which will be of benefit to everyone.

question Robert asks: 'The other day we were at a birthday party and before I knew it my son, who is a toddler, had polished off a whole bag of chips. He was really thirsty afterwards, drank a lot of water and wouldn't eat dinner that night. Is there a connection?'

answer If your baby or toddler has too much salted food he will increase his intake of fluids to quench his thirst. When this happens he will have little room left for food. Therefore, it is important to monitor your child's intake of salted foods on a day-to-day basis to minimise the chance of creating a fussy eater. In addition, it is recommended that fluids be served well prior to mealtimes so they do not replace healthy, nutritious meals.

7

ALLERGIES

While food allergies do not affect most babies, you need to be aware of them so you can minimise the risk of a reaction and also deal with any incident arising from a reaction, either in the case of your own baby or another in your care.

risk indicators

Allergies affect less than 10 per cent of babies and there are indicators that will assist you in determining whether your baby is in the risk category. Allergies are more likely to occur in babies with a family history of eczema, and when combined with other family conditions such as asthma and hay fever there is an increased probability your baby may be allergic to certain food groups.

high-allergy foods

Certain foods are more likely to cause an allergic reaction, including egg (especially the white), peanut products, cow's milk, strawberries, honey and some fish and shellfish. Even if your baby is not in the high-risk category, it is best to delay the introduction of these foods. This allows your baby's immune system to mature a little, thereby reducing the likelihood of an allergic reaction.

Egg yolks can be included in your baby's diet after six months and the whole egg from nine months. Other high-allergy foods should not be introduced until after your baby turns one. Where there is the potential for your baby to react to high-allergy foods, the length of the delay should be discussed with a health professional and will vary according to the likely severity of the reaction.

If you also follow the practice of introducing new foods in isolation it becomes reasonably easy to identify a problem food but if further help is required, seek advice from a doctor or dietician.

reactions

Depending on how severe the allergy is, reactions can vary from mild, an upset stomach, to extreme, such as an anaphylactic reaction where breathing is impeded. As a general rule, the more serious reactions occur quickly. Symptoms can include itching, swelling (mainly around the mouth), cramps, rashes, spots, vomiting and diarrhoea. Medical attention should be sought immediately for any extreme reaction.

tell everyone

If you know your baby is allergic to a particular food it is essential that everyone who cares for your child is made fully aware of the situation. This includes people such as your extended family, those at creches and child care centres, party hosts and friends.

growing out of allergies

Most children grow out of allergies as they get older, often at around the age of six years, but more severe cases, for example allergies to fish and peanuts, can be a lifelong problem.

question Rick asks: 'My wife has eczema and I have occasional bouts of mild asthma. Are we right to be concerned about our six-month-old twins having food allergies?'

answer Babies with a family history of eczema, asthma and hay fever are more likely to develop allergic reactions to certain foods. This does not necessarily mean the twins will have a problem, however, it is wise to be aware and to recognise the potential for a problem. Be careful when introducing certain high-allergy foods into the babies' diet.

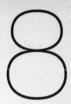

PRODUCT COMPARISONS

Regardless of how much of your baby's diet consists of home-cooked meals, most parents purchase some processed items, such as yoghurt, canned fruit and other staple foods. When you are doing this it is important to make comparisons across brands as they can vary significantly in terms of content.

As a very general rule, the cuter the packaging the worse the content. Often popular characters from books and television are featured prominently on the packaging to increase the product's appeal to babies and toddlers.

By becoming an avid label reader and comparing the important categories, such as sugar and salt, you will be able to select the best option for your baby. By law this information must be listed on the packaging and so long as you are comparing the same serving sizes it will prove most helpful.

The following comparisons in the categories of yoghurt, fruit juices, lunch items and dinner items illustrate how your baby will benefit from your detective work.

yoghurt

Yoghurt can be introduced into your baby's diet from the age of six months. It is not only convenient but is an excellent source of calcium, which is quickly absorbed by the body. When selecting yoghurt for your baby eliminate the low-fat and diet varieties. Choose a natural product as they have a lower sugar content than the flavoured alternatives. When comparing yoghurts, you should include some full-fat adult alternatives as they often have a lower sugar content than those produced specifically for the baby market.

Adding fresh fruit to natural yoghurt provides variety and naturally sweetens the taste. If your baby is already hooked on flavoured yoghurt and you would prefer them to have a natural product, offer them a blend of the two types for a week or so, then gradually shift the balance to the natural product.

fruit juices

Many parents believe that fruit juices are natural, healthy and a good source of vitamins for their baby but dieticians and nutritionists generally advise limiting juice as part of the daily diet. Instead they recommend babies enjoy milk, water and whole fruit, which will add some fibre to their diet as well as minimise the likelihood of diarrhoea, which can be the result of too much juice. In addition, due to the high concentration of sugars, fruit juice is a sweet drink of which babies may become a little too fond, and there is the risk they will fill up on juice leaving no room for food.

If your baby already drinks juice and you would like to wean them off it, do it by gradually adding water to their juice over time.

If you do choose to offer your baby a small amount of fruit juice it is important to compare the products on offer. Choose fruit juices that have no added preservatives or sugar. It is interesting to note that some adult juices can contain up to 50 per cent more sugar than those developed specifically for the baby market. In terms of dilution, manufacturers recommend a one-to-one ratio but it is preferable to mix one part juice to four parts water. In addition, the packaging on some juices states they are suitable for babies who are four months plus, but leaving it until your child is one year would be more appropriate.

lunch items

There is a large range of products to choose from in this section of the supermarket. On close examination common sense will tell you some choices will be better for your baby than others, for example canned fruit rather than chocolate mousse or creme caramel (which are available for babies from six months onwards).

Canned fruit is mostly produced with no added sugar, which means it contains natural rather than refined sugar. Obviously, fresh fruit has more nutritional value but canned fruit is convenient, especially when you are out and about, as it does not require refrigeration. In addition, canned fruit can be mixed with yoghurt, providing a reasonably nutritious meal for your baby.

dinner items

Although it is safe to say most parents at some point will have to rely on using a canned baby dinner, they should do so only occasionally. The comparison technique should provide the information you need to select the best option for your baby. There can be up to five times as much salt in some canned dinners when compared to others, so check the labels carefully.

HYGIENE HINTS

There are myriad strict rules and regulations that govern the workings of a commercial kitchen and although it might be impractical to apply these practices to your kitchen, you should make an extra effort at hygiene when the preparation of baby food is involved.

Micro-organisms are found in air, soil, water and food and they can have both desirable and undesirable effects. Among the desirable outcomes are that yeast will make bread rise, mould will enhance the flavour of certain cheeses, bacteria is of benefit in a yoghurt culture, and penicillin can assist with fighting bacterial infections. However, the major downside is that some micro-organisms can cause food poisoning, which can be serious for an adult but can have even more dire consequences for a baby.

Food poisoning occurs either because there is bacteria in the food itself, or because the food has been contaminated with a virus. Bacteria in food multiply at an alarming rate if the conditions are conducive. All bacteria need to thrive is time, warmth and moisture – given the chance, their numbers can double every

20 minutes to exceptionally dangerous levels. However, there are steps you can take to minimise the presence of micro-organisms in your kitchen and the food you prepare. The following advice will help you maintain safe food-handling and hygiene practices.

personal hygiene

Personal hygiene is of major importance in the kitchen as a lack of it can mean the transmission of viruses or bacteria. Although it seems like common sense, you should make it habit to wash and dry your hands thoroughly, preferably with a disposable towel, prior to cooking and handling food. Similarly, if you have a toddler helping in the kitchen you should ensure their hands are clean before you begin. It is also important that you do not prepare or cook food when you are feeling ill as germs can be easily transmitted to food through a cough or sneeze.

It is recommended that while in the kitchen you try to minimise contact with your hair, nose and ears as bacteria from these areas can be transferred to the food. In addition, if you have long hair it is best to tie it back. If you have any minor cuts or abrasions they should be treated and covered prior to handling food.

Most good cooks like to taste the fruits of their labour, often part way through the cooking process as well as at the end. When doing so, you should always use a tasting spoon that is kept separate and washed after each use. This ensures the dish is not contaminated by any bacteria that may be present in the mouth.

cleaning routine

Although you might not have the time and energy for a formal itemised cleaning routine, all equipment and utensils need to be washed and also disinfected on a regular basis. Crockery and cutlery should be washed in very hot, soapy water to avoid cross-contamination (using the dishwasher is fine). Sinks and benches should be washed and wiped down after you have finished cooking.

Chopping boards represent a major hazard as the small cracks that develop over time can be a haven for bacteria. Therefore, they should be scrubbed in hot, soapy water, and replaced regularly. A chopping board used in the preparation of raw meat should be meticulously cleaned before using it for any other task. Ideally, you should have a separate chopping board for raw meat and fish.

Floors should be swept and cleaned often to ensure germs and bacteria that have entered the kitchen on the soles of shoes are killed.

Tea towels should be laundered almost daily and washcloths should be replaced often. Tea towels and washcloths should never be used to clean up floor spills – use disposable towel instead.

storage

It is important to check your refrigerator is in top working order to ensure the safe storage of food. It should operate at a temperature of between one and five degrees Celsius. The seals should be checked often and you should never overcrowd the fridge as this will decrease the effectiveness of the airflow. Always cover food to be stored in the fridge and store raw food below cooked items. The fridge is the ideal place to defrost frozen foods as it means they spend no time in the temperature zone at which bacteria reproduce.

When freezing food you have cooked, do not allow it to cool on the bench overnight. Wait until the heat has reduced, then put it into the fridge for a while to cool down before transferring it to the freezer. It is important to cover, label and date the food being frozen and to follow any manufacturer's guidelines about the length of time the food may be stored.

When re-heating food it is important to bring the item to a boil or re-heat it to piping hot to kill off any bacteria that may be present.

Food scraps should be quickly placed in a rubbish bin with a lid, which should then be emptied frequently to prevent attracting pests and insects that have their own bacteria.

RECIPES

COOKING FOR YOUR BABY

The following recipes cover a variety of sweet and savoury dishes designed to provide healthy, nutritious meals that are easy to prepare. The majority of ingredients are probably already in your pantry; if not, they are readily available at the supermarket. While the reality is that we all use commercial alternatives from time to time (and the recipes that follow certainly allow for that), there's nothing like homemade pastry and so on. I have included, then, recipes for pastry, stock and crepes that are suitable for babies in the Basics section (see pages 58–64).

Some new parents are tempted to spend all day in the kitchen preparing complicated meals for their baby, but often the result is no more pleasing – or readily accepted – than that from a simple approach. Babies grow up so quickly that this time may be better spent taking them for a pram walk to the park or just having fun together. Remember: cooking for and feeding your baby should be enjoyable for everyone!

age groups

The recipes given here are divided into age groups. From my own experience with my little girl I have found this is the easiest way to be sure you are giving your baby the right foods at the right time. It also provides a practical reference that allows you to locate a suitable recipe quickly.

The age groups are 4–6 months, 6–9 months, 9–12 months and one year plus. The categories are narrow to allow for the inclusion of potential allergy foods, such as eggs, at the appropriate stage of your baby's development. Each age group represents a building block in your baby's diet. As they progress through each stage you will be able to add more and more to their menu. At the same time, it is important to recognise that although the texture of foods will change from group to group, there are recipes in the early sections that will still appeal to your baby when they are older.

serving size

The serving size, or the amount a recipe yields, appears directly below the recipe title. The serving size for a baby is an estimation as babies of a similar age can consume vastly different amounts of food. The family serve provides enough for two adults, a toddler and a baby.

washing and peeling

It is important to wash all fruit and vegetables prior to cooking or serving. Some vegetables, such as leeks, require more thorough washing but it is well worthwhile as the end result of your labours can be easily spoiled by small pieces of dirt or grit. The easiest way to wash leeks, or any vegetable that is to be blended, is to rinse the chopped vegetable in a colander under running water.

Don't forget to remove the strings from beans, snow peas and celery. I also don't include the stalks of broccoli or mushrooms as they are harder to deal with for babies.

Certain vegetables contain most of their nutritional value in their skin, for example zucchini and golden squash. It is advisable to cook such vegetables unpeeled, but they must be very well washed. Often the skin colour of these vegetables really enhances the appearance of a finished dish: we taste first with our eyes and so will your baby, as they quickly come to appreciate well-presented food .

seasoning

The recipes do not call for the use of seasonings, such as salt and pepper, and most use salt-reduced products, such as butter and stock. Young babies do not require much salt in their diet; too much can lead to a big thirst, which in turn can create a fussy eater. Too much salt can also significantly alter the taste of many foods.

blending and mashing

A number of the recipes require a blender. You may find that a hand-held blender is easier and more effective than a food processor when pureeing small quantities. Alternatively, you can use a fork to achieve a mash consistency.

additional features

This symbol indicates a toddler task. The associated information is for those of you with toddlers who are old enough to help with simple tasks in the kitchen. Even though it is more time consuming, I always encourage this practice as it often leads to the toddler being really interested in the food they have helped cook and, therefore, more likely to eat it. There is also the added amusement value for the toddler.

Recipes marked with this symbol can be converted into a family meal for those nights when you start to think about your own dinner far too late and end up having not much or skipping it altogether. Or on the happy, albeit rare, occasions that you can all sit down as a family. While not always practical, eating together helps develop good eating habits.

In either case, the bonus is that you don't have to cook two meals!

daily menu guide

The following table provides an example of a typical baby's daily menu at each stage, and can be used to help you plan your own baby's menu.

Daily guide	4–6 months	6–9 months	9–12 months	One year plus
texture stage	purees & smooth mashes	fork-mashes	large diced food & finger food	chewy finger food & 'family food'
average milk feeds	5	4	3	3
average milk intake	900 ml	700 ml	700 ml	600 ml
early morning	breast milk or formula	breast milk or formula	breast milk or formula	–
breakfast	rice cereal	rice cereal with fruit or baby muesli *then* breast milk or formula	cereal, muesli, french toast or oats and apple	cereal, scrambled egg or muffins *then* milk
mid morning	breast milk or formula	–	cheese twists, rusks or fruit pieces *then* water	pumpkin loaf or fresh fruit
lunch	breast milk or formula *then* fruit puree, mash or gel	apple & ricotta combo or nutmeg nectarine *then* breast milk or formula	cheese omelette, sandwich or baked pear custard *then* breast milk or formula	vegetable frittata or chicken & corn parcels *then* milk
afternoon	–	rusks	fruit gel or cruskits *then* water	avocado cherry tomatoes or baby muesli biscuits
dinner	breast milk or formula *then* vegetable puree, mash, soup or risotto	sweet potato pie, beef & udon noodles or tuna mornay	zucchini cheese slice, pork & apple croquets or salmon pasta	hearty beef pie or stir-fry pork noodles *then* water
before bedtime	breast milk or formula	breast milk or formula	breast milk or formula	milk

BASICS

Most new parents have very little spare time in their day, so I have included in this section recipes for stock, pastry and crepes that can be made in advance and refrigerated or frozen for later use. By preparing these basics when you do have spare time, you'll still be able to whip up a homemade nutritious meal when you don't!

baby beef stock

makes 2 litres

olive oil

300 g chuck or casserole steak

1 carrot, chopped

1 small piece leek, chopped

1 stalk celery, chopped

3 litres water

Preheat the oven to 180°C and lightly oil a medium-sized baking dish. Trim any excess fat from the meat and cut the meat into cubes. Transfer the meat to the dish and bake for 20 minutes until browned. Remove from the oven and drain off any fat. Place the meat in a medium-sized stockpot. Place the vegetables in the baking dish and toss with a little olive oil. Bake for 20 minutes. Remove from the oven and add to the stock pot. Add the water and simmer gently on the stovetop for 2 hours, stirring occasionally. Allow to cool and skim off any fat on the surface. Strain through a fine sieve. Refrigerate, or freeze for up to 2 months.

toddler task
Wash the vegetables.

family meal
Use the beef stock in risotto, casseroles, sauces and soups.

baby chicken stock

makes 1 litre

1 small chicken carcass

2 litres water

1 carrot, chopped

1 small piece leek, chopped

1 stalk celery, chopped

¼ cup parsley

Trim any excess fat from the chicken and place the carcass into a medium-sized stockpot. Add the water and bring to a boil, then skim off any fat on the surface. Add the vegetables and parsley and simmer gently for 90 minutes, stirring occasionally. Remove from the heat, discard the chicken carcass and allow the stock to cool. Skim off any fat and strain the stock through a fine sieve. Refrigerate, or freeze for up to 2 months.

toddler task

Wash the vegetables and the parsley.

family meal

Use the chicken stock in risotto, casseroles, soups and sauces.

sweet shortcrust pastry

makes 500 g

200 g plain flour
150 g icing sugar
150 g unsalted butter, softened
1 egg

Sift the flour and icing sugar into a large bowl. Using your fingertips, rub the butter into the dry ingredients until the mixture resembles breadcrumbs. Add the egg and mix to form a dough. Turn the dough out onto a floured board and knead lightly until smooth. Roll the dough into a ball, then cover with cling wrap and refrigerate for 1 hour prior to use or freeze for up to 3 months.

Note: The recipes in this book call for '1 sheet shortcrust pastry' or similar, in recognition of the fact that the commercial product is so widely used. The above recipe will make the equivalent of about 2 sheets. If desired, freeze the dough in 2 portions, for ease of handling.

savoury shortcrust pastry

makes 400 g

250 g plain flour
pinch of salt
125 g butter, softened and diced
50 ml cold water

Sift the flour into a large bowl and add the salt and butter. Using your fingertips, rub the butter into the dry ingredients until the mixture resembles very fine breadcrumbs. Add most of the water and mix to form a dough, adding more water if required. Turn the dough out onto a floured board and knead lightly until smooth. Roll the dough into a ball, then cover with cling wrap and refrigerate for 1 hour prior to use or freeze for up to 3 months.

Note: The recipes in this book call for '1 sheet shortcrust pastry' or similar, in recognition of the fact that the commercial product is so widely used. The above recipe will make the equivalent of about 2 sheets. If desired, freeze the dough in 2 portions, for ease of handling.

savoury crepes

makes 12

125 g plain flour

small pinch of salt

1 egg

1 cup milk

25 g butter, melted

Sift the flour and salt into a large bowl. Make a well in the centre, then add the egg and mix together. Add the milk, whisking constantly to produce a smooth batter. Slowly whisk in the butter and allow the batter to stand for 1 hour prior to use. Pour a little of the batter into a heated, lightly oiled, non-stick frypan and cook over a low heat for 1 minute or so until lightly coloured, then flip the crepe over and cook the other side. Transfer to disposable towel to drain and continue cooking the crepes.

Note: These crepes can be made the day before they are required and refrigerated covered with cling wrap.

sweet crepes

makes 12

125 g plain flour
small pinch of salt
1 egg
1½ tablespoons caster sugar
1 cup milk
25 g butter

Sift the flour and salt into a large bowl. Make a well in the centre, then add the egg and sugar and mix together. Add the milk, whisking constantly to produce a smooth batter. Cook the butter in a small saucepan over medium heat until nut brown, then whisk it into the batter. Allow the batter to stand for 1 hour before using. Pour a little batter into a heated, lightly oiled, non-stick frypan and cook over a low heat for 1 minute or so until lightly coloured, then flip the crepe over and cook the other side. Transfer to disposable towel to drain and continue cooking the crepes.

Note: These crepes can be made the day before they are required and refrigerated covered with cling wrap.

4–6 MONTHS

After the initial excitement of introducing their baby to solid food, many parents tell me they feel guilty for not offering a different menu at every meal. The truth is that there are a limited number of options available to you at this puree and smooth-mash stage. In fact, *you* are far more likely to get bored with the repetition before your baby. Nevertheless, the following recipes should provide both of you with sufficient variety to get you through the first couple of months, after which the menu expands considerably.

It is customary to begin by offering your baby savoury foods, such as potato and pumpkin, following them with sweeter flavours, such as apple and pear. In this early stage, it is wise to offer foods in isolation as this helps to identify any allergy-causing foods. The following list of ideas for savoury and sweet purees should be enough to keep you going during the initial period. Once your baby has tried various foods on their own with no side effects, it is appropriate to offer them the combined dishes in this section.

ideas for purees and mashes

Savoury	Sweet
avocado	apple
carrot	apricot
parsnip	banana
potato	blueberry
pumpkin	mango
squash	nectarine
swede	peach
sweet corn	pear
sweet potato	plum
turnip	raspberry
zucchini	rhubarb

carrot and rice puree
makes 4 baby portions

2 carrots, peeled and chopped
¼ cup rice, washed
400 ml water

Place carrots and rice in a medium-sized saucepan. Add the water and cover. Cook over a medium heat for 20 minutes. Allow to cool, then blend to a puree or smooth-mash consistency.

baby vegetable soup

makes 1 family portion

1 zucchini, sliced

2 golden squash, sliced

1 potato, peeled and diced

1 sweet potato, peeled and diced

1 carrot, peeled and sliced

¼ cup jasmine rice, washed

1 litre water

Put all the ingredients into a large saucepan. Cover and bring to a boil, then gently simmer for 30 minutes. Allow the mixture to cool, then blend until smooth.

For a thicker consistency, drain off some of the liquid prior to blending.

toddler task
Wash the rice under cold running water.

family meal
Serve the soup sprinkled with freshly chopped parsley and cracked black pepper and with some warm crusty bread.

pumpkin and noodle puree

makes 4 baby portions

200 g butternut pumpkin, peeled and chopped

50 g dried noodles

2 cups water

Put all the ingredients into a saucepan. Cover and cook over a medium heat. After 5 minutes use a fork to break up the softened noodles. Cook for a further 15 minutes until the pumpkin is soft. Allow to cool, then drain off the liquid and blend to a puree or smooth-mash consistency.

swede and sweet potato risotto

makes 1 family portion

1 tablespoon salt-reduced butter

1 swede, peeled and chopped

1 sweet potato, peeled and chopped

1 cup arborio rice, washed

1 litre water

Melt half the butter in a medium-sized saucepan and add the swede and sweet potato. Cover and cook over a medium heat for 15 minutes. Remove the vegetables from the pan and set aside. Melt the remaining butter in the pan, add the rice and cook over a medium heat for 2 minutes, stirring constantly. Return the vegetables to the pan and combine with the rice. Add 400 ml of the water and stir occasionally. When the water has been absorbed add another 300 ml.

Repeat this process with the remaining water and simmer over a low heat until the rice is cooked. Allow the mixture to cool, then blend to a puree or smooth-mash consistency, adding a little more water if a thinner risotto is required.

toddler task

Wash the rice under cold running water.

family meal

Set aside some of the risotto prior to blending, stir through a little cream and serve as an accompaniment to a main meal.

rice cereal and sweet potato puree

makes 2 baby portions

100 g sweet potato, peeled and chopped

220 ml water

2 tablespoons baby rice cereal

Place the sweet potato and 200 ml of the water in a saucepan. Cover
and cook over a low heat for 10 minutes. Allow to cool, then blend
to a puree or smooth-mash consistency. In a separate bowl, combine the remaining water and the rice cereal and stir until smooth.
Add the sweet potato puree and combine well. Serve warm.

toddler task

Mix the rice cereal and water to a smooth texture.

parsnip and potato puree

makes 2 baby portions

1 parsnip, peeled and chopped

1 potato, peeled and chopped

1¼ cups water

Put all the ingredients into a saucepan. Cover and simmer gently for 20 minutes until the vegetables are soft. Remove from heat and drain off half the liquid. Allow the remaining liquid and vegetables to cool, then blend to a puree or smooth-mash consistency.

baked pumpkin puree

makes 2 baby portions

200 g butternut pumpkin, peeled and chopped

olive oil

¼ cup water

Preheat the oven to 180°C. Place the pumpkin in a small, lightly oiled baking dish and bake for 30 minutes. Remove from the oven and allow to cool. Blend the pumpkin and water to a puree or smooth-mash consistency.

potato and leek puree

makes 2 baby portions

1 potato, peeled and chopped
1 × 5 cm piece leek, sliced
1½ cups water

Put all the ingredients into a saucepan. Cover and cook over a medium heat for 15 minutes. Remove from heat and drain off half the liquid. Allow the remaining liquid and vegetables to cool, then blend to a puree or smooth-mash consistency.

pumpkin and chickpea puree

makes 2 baby portions

200 g pumpkin, peeled and chopped
¼ cup canned chickpeas, drained and washed
1 cup water

Put all the ingredients into a saucepan. Cover and cook over a low heat for 15 minutes. Allow to cool, then blend to a puree or smooth-mash consistency.

toddler task
Drain the chickpeas and wash under running water.

spinach and potato puree

makes 2 baby portions

2 potatoes, peeled and chopped

1 small handful spinach, chopped

1 cup water

Put all the ingredients into a saucepan. Cover and cook over a low heat for 15 minutes. Remove from heat and drain off half the liquid. Allow the remaining liquid and vegetables to cool, then blend to a puree or smooth-mash consistency.

toddler task

Wash the spinach.

butter bean and rice puree

makes 2 baby portions

200 g canned butter beans, drained and washed

20 g rice, washed

1¼ cups water

Place the butter beans, rice and two thirds of the water in a saucepan. Cover and cook over a low heat for 15 minutes. Allow the mixture to cool, then add the remaining water and blend to a puree or smooth-mash consistency.

peach and mango fruit gel

makes 2 baby portions

10 g gelatine
1 cup boiling water
80 g pureed peach
80 g pureed mango

In a bowl, sprinkle the gelatine onto the boiling water and stir thoroughly to ensure it dissolves completely. Add the pureed fruit and stir to combine. Pour into a small dish, allow to cool slightly, then refrigerate overnight.

toddler task

Help to puree the fruit by mashing it with a fork.

family meal

Serve fruit gel topped with slices of fresh peach or mango with a scoop of fresh cream. Garnish with fresh mint.

*celebrity tip

from Georgie Parker, award-winning actor and star of *All Saints*
My kitchen speciality for my baby is mashed vegetables: parsnip, zucchini, pumpkin, broccoli and peas. Simple, healthy and she enjoys it – on a good day!

6–9 MONTHS

At this stage most parents say it is hard to believe how far their baby has come in such a short space of time. Just two months ago they were on a liquid diet and already they are moving into the second stage of solid food. By now your baby will have mastered the physical actions of swallowing and chewing, which enables them to progress from pureed food to fork-mashed food. This poses a challenge for some babies at first until they get used to the new texture. If you try fork-mashed food and your baby is constantly gagging, return to purees and try again a few days later. Slowly but surely is the recommended approach. Try not to worry if your baby seems to be progressing more slowly than other babies – eventually they *will* get there.

As your baby grows they will get more teeth, which is good news for solid food but not so enjoyable for a breastfeeding mother. Your baby's appetite for food will increase as their stomach grows and it is during this time that the balance usually swings from milk towards solid food. It is important to remember, however, that milk is of vital importance in your baby's diet, particularly in their first year, so you must ensure they are receiving the appropriate amount. For this age group this is approximately 700 ml daily.

Babies who are 6–9 months old and who do not have allergies are now able to try egg yolk. When first giving your baby egg yolk it is wise to serve only a small amount. Add half a teaspoon of crumbled hard-boiled yolk to some vegetables and carefully observe as your baby eats, to ensure there is no adverse reaction. See page 27 for more information about eggs and allergies.

Full-cream dairy milk can now be used in small amounts in cooking, which can start to make life a little easier because you can use milk on cereal and in other dishes, such as a white sauce. If your baby has an allergy it is wise to delay the introduction of cow's milk until they are a little older. When introducing cow's milk into the diet, do it gradually by blending it with their regular type of milk for a couple of days.

The time is now right to introduce red meat into your baby's diet and it is also appropriate to include poultry and fish for this age group. Having tried once without success many parents think their babies do not like the taste of meat, poultry and fish but most often the baby is objecting to the texture. Therefore, if you make a little extra effort to blend the finished dish to the appropriate texture for your baby they should enjoy the new additions to their daily fare.

Your baby is becoming aware of colours at this time and therefore it helps to consider how appetising their food looks. Just like adults do, babies taste first with their eyes and if food looks appealing there is a greater chance they will want to try it.

homemade rusks

makes 18

olive oil
6 slices wholemeal toast bread
Vegemite
¼ cup grated cheddar cheese

Preheat the oven to 150°C and lightly oil a flat baking tray. Remove the crusts from the bread, then spread only 3 of the slices with a thin layer of Vegemite. Cut each of the 6 slices into 3 fingers and place on the tray. Bake in the oven for 50 minutes, then remove and sprinkle the cheese on the Vegemite rusks only. Return to the oven for a further 10 minutes until the rusks are crispy and the cheese has melted. Cool on a wire rack and store in an airtight container for up to 3 days.

baby pumpkin soup

makes 1 family portion

1 tablespoon salt-reduced butter

1 onion, diced

300 g butternut pumpkin, peeled and chopped

2 cups salt-reduced chicken stock

Melt the butter in a medium-sized saucepan. Add the onion and cook over a medium heat for 5 minutes until transparent. Add the pumpkin, then cover and cook over a low heat for 10 minutes, stirring occasionally. Pour in the chicken stock, then replace the lid and cook for a further 30 minutes. Allow to cool, then blend to a soup consistency.

family meal

Stir through some thickened cream and freshly chopped parsley to create a sauce for veal ravioli. Serve topped with grated parmesan cheese. Offer garlic bread, too, for a more hearty meal.

tuna mornay

makes 1 family portion

100 g salt-reduced butter
100 g plain flour
3 cups milk
1 × 180 g can tuna in springwater
½ cup grated cheddar cheese

Slowly melt the butter in a large saucepan, then stir in the flour with a wooden spoon. Once combined, cook over a low heat for 2 minutes, stirring constantly. Still over a low heat, slowly whisk in the milk to produce a smooth white sauce. Add the tuna and its liquid and the cheese to the sauce and stir until it thickens.

toddler task
Break up the canned tuna with a fork and 'double check' there are no bones.

family meal
Spoon the tuna mixture into vol au vent cases, sprinkle with some grated cheese and bake in a moderate oven until warmed through and the cheese has melted. Serve with a crisp green salad tossed with an olive oil and balsamic vinegar dressing.

potato, leek and broccoli soup

makes 1 family portion

1 tablespoon salt-reduced butter

1 × 5 cm piece leek, sliced

1 potato, peeled and chopped

150 g broccoli, chopped

1½ cups salt-reduced chicken stock

Melt the butter in a large saucepan. Add the leek and sauté over a medium heat until soft but not coloured, about 5 minutes. Add the potato and broccoli, then cover and cook over a low heat for 10 minutes, stirring occasionally. Pour in the chicken stock and cook for a further 30 minutes. Allow to cool, then blend to a smooth consistency.

toddler task

Wash the leek and broccoli and separate the broccoli florets from the stems by snapping them off.

beef and udon noodles

makes 2 baby portions

100 g fillet steak, finely sliced

1 cup salt-reduced beef stock

1 cup canned crushed tomatoes

200 g udon noodles

Place the fillet steak and the stock in a medium-sized saucepan and bring to a boil. Reduce the heat to low, then cover with a lid and cook for 10 minutes. Add the tomatoes and noodles and cook for a further 5 minutes. Allow the mixture to cool, then blend to required consistency.

sweet potato pie

makes 4 baby portions

olive oil

200 g sweet potato, peeled and chopped

½ cup water

½ cup cottage cheese

¼ cup baby muesli

salt-reduced butter

Preheat the oven to 180°C and lightly oil a small baking dish. Place the sweet potato and water in a saucepan. Cover and cook over a low heat for 10 minutes. Allow to cool, then drain and mash with a fork. Stir in the cottage cheese and transfer the mixture to the baking dish. Top with the baby muesli and dot with shavings of butter. Bake for 15 minutes, until the topping is golden.

toddler task

Mash the sweet potato with a fork.

chicken and sweet corn soup

makes 1 family portion

200 g minced chicken

200 g creamed corn

50 g small shell pasta

2 cups salt-reduced chicken stock

Place all the ingredients in a large saucepan and stir with a wooden spoon to break up the chicken and combine the ingredients. Bring to a boil, then cover and cook over a low heat for 20 minutes. Allow the mixture to cool slightly, then blend, leaving some texture.

 family meal

Serve soup with a sprinkling of parsley for a hearty lunch.

cauliflower with cheese sauce

makes 2 baby portions

olive oil

200 g cauliflower, chopped

50 g salt-reduced butter

50 g plain flour

1½ cups milk

¼ cup grated cheddar cheese

Preheat the oven to 180°C and lightly oil a small baking dish. Arrange the pieces of cauliflower closely together in a layer in the baking dish.

Slowly melt the butter in a large saucepan, then stir in the flour with a wooden spoon. Once combined, cook over a low heat for 2 minutes, stirring constantly. Slowly whisk in the milk to produce a smooth white sauce. Add the grated cheese and stir through.

Cover the cauliflower generously with the cheese sauce and bake, uncovered, for 20 minutes. Remove from the oven and allow to cool, then blend to the required consistency.

family meal
Make this in a larger quantity and serve it (unblended!) with your favourite roast.

avocado mousse

makes 6

olive oil

2 avocados, mashed

8 tablespoons sour cream

1 tablespoon lemon juice

10 g gelatine

½ cup boiling water

Lightly oil 6 individual moulds or a small dish. Combine the avocado, sour cream and lemon juice in a bowl, mixing well. In a separate bowl, sprinkle the gelatine onto the boiling water and stir thoroughly to ensure it dissolves completely. Slowly whisk the dissolved gelatine into the avocado mixture. Pour into the moulds and refrigerate overnight. To turn out each mousse, dip the base of the mould in hot water and invert it over a plate.

toddler task

Mash the avocado with a fork.

apple and ricotta combo

makes 2 baby portions

1 apple, peeled and diced

½ cup water

¼ cup smooth ricotta cheese

Place the apple and water in a saucepan and cook for 10 minutes until the apple is soft. Allow to cool, then mash or blend to the required consistency. Add the ricotta cheese, mix well, then refrigerate. Serve cold.

toddler task

Mash the apple with a fork.

baked bananas

makes 2 baby portions

olive oil

1 banana

¼ cup orange juice

1 tablespoon natural yoghurt

Preheat the oven to 180°C and lightly oil a small baking dish. Cut the banana in half and then slice each half lengthways. Shave a small amount of fruit off the base of each piece so it sits flat in the dish. Lie the fruit in the dish, then pour over the orange juice and bake for 20 minutes, carefully turning the bananas once during the cooking process. Allow the bananas to cool slightly, then remove them to a plate. Mix the yoghurt into the remaining juice in the baking dish and pour over the warm bananas. Mash or blend to the required consistency and serve warm.

mango and cream cheese spread

makes 1 family portion

1 mango, peeled and stoned
250 g cream cheese, softened

Mash the mango with a fork, then mix with the cream cheese.
Transfer the mixture to a small dish, then cover and refrigerate
overnight. Spread onto homemade rusks (see page 77) or Cruskits.

toddler task
Mash the mango to a puree consistency with a fork.

family meal
Preheat the oven to 220°C. Using a sharp knife, cut a pocket in the
thickest part of a skinless chicken breast. Spoon in some of
the mango and cream cheese mixture and use a toothpick to close
the pocket. Coat the chicken breast with seasoned flour, then cook
in a heated, oiled non-stick frypan over a medium heat until lightly
browned. Transfer to the oven for approximately 20 minutes to
finish the cooking.

nutmeg nectarines

makes 4

olive oil

4 nectarines, stoned and diced

1 teaspoon nutmeg

Preheat the oven to 160°C and lightly oil a small baking dish. Place the nectarine in the dish and sprinkle with nutmeg. Cook for 20 minutes, until soft, and serve warm or cold with a scoop of natural yoghurt.

*celebrity tip

from Iain Hewitson, restaurateur, chef and author

Charlotte is a little young, as yet, for me to conduct any great culinary experiments. But my mother always told me that when all else failed I would eat a rough mash of equal quantities of carrot, parsnip and apple with a little knob of butter, and on special occasions a splash of gravy.

9–12 MONTHS

At 9 months it can feel like just yesterday that your baby did little but drink milk and sleep, and now – all of a sudden – they do not stay still for long. This increase in physical activity produces a higher energy requirement. Rolling, crawling and walking all take enormous effort, particularly during the learning phase, and your baby's diet needs to provide them with enough fuel to accomplish these tasks.

As their strength grows, the texture of their food can progress to large diced food, and finger food will become popular as they perfect their hand–eye coordination.

Snacks are necessary to provide a boost in energy levels throughout the day, but they must be healthy to do the job properly. Snacks should not be given too close to mealtimes as they will leave little room for proper meals.

Babies of this age often also have an increased water intake, especially in warmer weather, but you need to ensure they are not filling up with liquid too close to mealtimes as again this will interfere with appetite.

Whole eggs can be introduced to the diet at this stage, as long as your baby does not have any food allergies so far and is not in a high-risk group (see page 40). A good method of introducing a whole egg is to offer your baby a tablespoon or so of scrambled egg and observe closely to ensure it agrees with them. Once you have done this successfully, egg can be used in many dishes and the menu will broaden considerably to include things like custards, pikelets, muffins and omelettes. Not only are eggs an excellent source of protein but they are also convenient, and can make a quick and nutritious meal.

ideas for finger food

- homemade rusks with Vegemite (see page 77)
- Ripe fruit, such as banana fingers; mango, pear, peach and nectarine slices; watermelon and cantaloupe balls; orange segments; grated apple; skinned and halved grapes; apricot halves
- Parcooked vegetables such as zucchini fingers, carrot rounds, sweet potato ribbons, golden squash slices, celery and cucumber matches, and broccoli florets
- Toss cooked pasta such as pumpkin gnocchi, spinach trivelle, tomato fusilli or orecchiette with a little olive oil
- Soaked (overnight to soften) and chopped dried fruits such as apricots, apples and sultanas
- Sliced hard-boiled egg
- Cheddar-cheese sticks and slices
- Cruskits
- Sandwiches, such as finger, ribbon and pinwheel

french toast

makes 1 baby portion

1 slice toast bread

1 egg

¼ cup milk

1 tablespoon grated cheddar cheese

20 g salt-reduced butter

Remove the crusts from the bread and cut the slice into squares. In a small bowl, mix the egg and milk together with a fork. Add the cheese, stir, then dip the bread into the mixture and coat well.

Heat the butter in a non-stick frypan and cook the squares over a medium heat for 10 minutes until golden brown on both sides.

toddler task

Crack the egg; add the grated cheese; stir the mixture.

creamy oats and apple

makes 4 baby portions

½ cup one-minute oats

1 cup milk

140 g pureed apple

Place the oats and milk in a small saucepan, then stir and bring to a boil. Reduce the heat, then add the apple puree and cook for 1 minute, stirring constantly until the mixture has thickened. Serve warm.

toddler task

Measure the oats.

stewed rhubarb and yoghurt

makes 2 baby portions

100 g rhubarb, peeled and chopped

1 cup water

¼ cup caster sugar

⅓ cup natural yoghurt

Place the rhubarb in a saucepan and add the water. Cover and cook over a low heat for 10 minutes. Add the sugar and cook, uncovered, for a further 5 minutes, stirring constantly. Allow to cool, then drain off half the liquid and blend until smooth. Mix with the yoghurt and refrigerate. Serve cold.

scrambled eggs

makes 1 baby portion

2 eggs

¼ cup milk

1 teaspoon salt-reduced butter

Beat the eggs and milk in a small bowl, with a fork. Melt the butter over a medium heat in a non-stick frypan. Pour the egg mixture into the pan and stir with a wooden spoon to scramble it. Cook for a further 5 minutes until the egg has set.

toddler task

Crack the eggs and beat the mixture with a fork.

baby rice cereal pikelets

makes 24

2 eggs

50 g iron-enriched baby rice cereal

100 ml milk

50 g salt-reduced butter

Whisk the eggs in a large mixing bowl, then stir in the rice cereal and milk. Mix to a smooth dough-like consistency. Melt a teaspoon of the butter in a non-stick frypan. Drop small amounts of the mixture into the pan and cook slowly over a low heat until golden brown on both sides. Repeat until all the mixture has been used.

For sweet pikelets add some pureed fruit, such as mango, apple or pear, to the mixture prior to cooking. For savoury pikelets replace the fruit with grated zucchini, cheese or tomato paste.

toddler task

Pour the milk into the pikelet mixture; mash the fresh fruit with a fork.

cheese omelette

makes 1 baby portion

2 eggs
¼ cup milk
1 teaspoon salt-reduced butter
¼ cup grated cheddar cheese

In a small bowl, beat the eggs and milk lightly with a fork. Melt the butter over a medium heat in a non-stick frypan. Pour the mixture into the pan and sprinkle the cheese on top. Cook for 5 minutes until the egg has just set. Finish off the omelette by placing the pan under a hot griller for 1 minute until the cheese is golden.

toddler task
Beat the egg and milk together.

chicken risoni

makes 1 family portion

1 litre water

olive oil

100 g risoni pasta

200 g minced chicken

100 g zucchini, grated

6 basil leaves, torn

30 g salt-reduced butter

2 tablespoons plain flour

1 cup salt-reduced chicken stock

½ cup thickened cream

Boil the water in a large saucepan with a drop of olive oil. Add the risoni and cook for 15 minutes, stirring occasionally. Drain the pasta, then toss in a little olive oil. Sauté the chicken in an oiled non-stick frypan over a medium heat for 15 minutes, using a wooden spoon to break up the meat during cooking. Remove and set aside. Add a little oil to the heated pan and sauté the zucchini and basil until soft. Combine this with the chicken in a large bowl and add the risoni.

Slowly melt the butter in a large saucepan, then stir in the flour with a wooden spoon. Once combined, cook over a low heat for 2 minutes, stirring constantly. Slowly whisk in the chicken stock to produce a smooth sauce and cook gently until thickened. Remove from the heat and stir through the cream. Add the sauce to the chicken risoni mixture and blend, if required.

toddler task

Wash the zucchini and basil; measure the risoni.

family meal

Place the chicken risoni mixture in a lightly oiled, medium-sized baking dish. Top with grated cheddar cheese, parmesan cheese and cracked black pepper. Bake at 180°C until heated through and the cheese is golden, about 20 minutes. Serve with herb bread.

*celebrity tip

from Jackie Quist, television journalist and reporter

Chicken Bambino is a life saver for busy working mums trying to tempt fussy babies. My two children both loved this recipe and it can be prepared quickly, divided into small portions and frozen.

chicken bambino

Place a skinless chicken breast in a container with a dash of water. Cover and microwave on high for approximately 2 minutes until cooked through. Roughly chop into cubes a handful of broccoli, 3 golden squash, 1 peeled carrot and 1 small peeled potato. Place the vegetables in a covered container and microwave on high for 4 minutes until they are soft. Other vegies can be used and polenta can be substituted for the potato for something a little different. Shred the chicken into small pieces and add to the cooked vegies. Blend or puree if required, add a dash of Vegemite – and voilà!

pork and apple croquets

makes 24

200 g minced pork	1 apple, peeled and grated
2 cups water	½ cup plain flour
1 potato, boiled and mashed	1 egg, lightly beaten
1 tablespoon milk	½ cup breadcrumbs
2 egg yolks	olive oil

Poach the minced pork by placing it and the water in a saucepan and gently simmering with the lid on for 15 minutes. Use a wooden spoon to break up the meat during cooking. Drain and set the meat aside. Allow the mince to cool. In a large bowl, combine the mashed potato, milk, egg yolks and apple, mixing well. Refrigerate for 30 minutes. Add the pork and, using floured hands, mould the mixture into small croquet shapes. Roll each croquet in flour, then dip into the beaten egg and coat with breadcrumbs. Heat some oil in a non-stick frypan over a medium heat and cook the croquets until they are golden brown, about 10 minutes. Drain on disposable towel.

toddler task
Help crumb the croquets.

family meal
Make larger croquets and serve with cranberry sauce, creamy mashed potato and green beans.

summer vegetable gnocchi

makes 1 family portion

olive oil

50 g broccoli florets, chopped

50 g snow peas, thinly sliced

1 zucchini, diced

2 golden squash, diced

3 cups canned crushed tomatoes

2 tablespoons tomato paste

2 litres water

500 g gnocchi

Heat a little oil in a medium-sized non-stick frypan and sauté the broccoli and snow peas over a medium heat for 10 minutes. Add the zucchini and squash and cook for a further 5 minutes. Add the tomato, stir through the tomato paste and simmer for 15 minutes, stirring occasionally. Meanwhile, bring the water to a boil in a large saucepan and add a drop of olive oil. Add the gnocchi and cook until they rise to the surface. Drain and serve topped with the vegetable sauce.

toddler task

Wash the fresh vegetables.

tuna and corn balls

makes 18

100 g canned tuna chunks in springwater, drained and flaked
½ cup canned creamed corn
1 cup cooked rice
½ cup plain flour
1 egg, lightly beaten
½ cup breadcrumbs
olive oil

Put the tuna, corn and rice into a large bowl and mix together well. Using floured hands, mould the tuna mixture into small balls. Roll each ball in flour, then dip into the egg and coat with breadcrumbs. Heat some oil in a non-stick frypan and cook the balls over a medium heat for 10 minutes until golden.

toddler task

Flake the tuna; beat the egg with a fork; roll the tuna and corn balls in breadcrumbs.

salmon pasta

makes 1 family portion

1 × 210 g can pink salmon

1 litre water

olive oil

100 g small shell pasta

100 g salt-reduced butter

100 g plain flour

3 cups salt-reduced vegetable stock

½ cup thickened cream

½ cup grated cheddar cheese

50 g peas, cooked

Drain the salmon and carefully remove the dark flesh and bones, then flake through with a fork. Bring the water to a boil in a large saucepan with a drop of olive oil and add the pasta. Cook for 15 minutes, stirring occasionally, until al dente. Drain the pasta, toss with a little olive oil and set aside. Slowly melt the butter in a large saucepan, then stir in the flour with a wooden spoon. Once combined, cook over a low heat for 2 minutes, stirring constantly. Slowly whisk in the stock to produce a smooth sauce. Add the cream and cheese and cook for a further 3 minutes. Add the salmon and peas, then stir and serve poured over the pasta.

toddler task

Flake through the salmon to check all bones have been removed.

chicken, cheese and basil balls

makes 32

500 g minced chicken
200 g cheddar cheese, grated
6 basil leaves, finely chopped
1 egg
1 cup breadcrumbs
olive oil

Put the minced chicken, cheese, basil and egg into a bowl and mix together well. Using your hands, mould the mixture into small balls and coat with breadcrumbs. Heat a little oil in a non-stick frypan and cook the balls over a medium heat until golden brown, about 15 minutes.

toddler task
Coat the balls with breadcrumbs.

family meal
Place some of the chicken mixture in the centre of half a sheet of puff pastry. Fold the pastry over the mixture once and fold in both ends. Fold over again to form a parcel and pinch the edges together. Brush with melted butter and bake at 180°C for 30 minutes. Serve with a mango sauce or chutney.

savoury potatoes

makes 2 baby portions

olive oil

1 potato, peeled and thinly sliced

1 sweet potato, peeled and thinly sliced

½ cup milk

½ cup thickened cream

1 teaspoon nutmeg

Preheat the oven to 180°C and lightly oil a small baking dish. Layer the potato on the base of the dish and top with the sweet potato. In a small jug, mix the cream and the milk together and pour over the potatoes. Sprinkle the nutmeg on top and place the dish on a flat baking tray. Bake in the oven for 45 minutes.

toddler task

Mix the cream and milk together; sprinkle on the nutmeg.

family meal

Increase the quantities and serve this delicious dish alongside grilled pork, lamb or chicken.

pumpkin polenta

makes 16 shapes

3 cups water

1 cup polenta

100 g pureed pumpkin

olive oil

Bring the water to a boil in a large saucepan and slowly add the polenta. Cook uncovered over a low heat, stirring constantly, until the polenta takes on a porridge-like consistency. Remove from the heat and stir through the pumpkin. Spoon into a lightly oiled, shallow dish and smooth the top. Refrigerate until set, then cut into fingers, triangles or any other shape. Heat some oil in a non-stick frypan and cook the polenta pieces over a low heat to warm them through prior to serving.

 family meal

Serve polenta fingers alongside some grilled chicken or lamb.

zucchini and cheese slice

makes 16 slices

olive oil

4 eggs

½ cup milk

300 g zucchini, grated

1 cup grated cheddar cheese

½ cup plain flour

Preheat the oven to 180°C and lightly oil a small ovenproof dish. Put the eggs and milk into a large bowl and mix well. Add the zucchini and cheese, then stir in the flour. Pour into the baking dish and place in the oven. Cook for 40 minutes until golden brown. Allow to cool slightly before slicing.

toddler task

Crack the eggs; help to grate the zucchini.

family meal

Serve with a leafy salad for a delicious lunch, or, alternatively, make this using a muffin tray. Great on picnics!

cheese twists

makes 18

olive oil

1 sheet puff pastry

½ cup grated cheddar cheese

20 g salt-reduced butter, melted

Preheat the oven to 180°C and lightly oil a flat baking tray. Cut the pastry sheet into thirds, then each third into 6 strips. Place a small amount of cheese along the middle of each strip of pastry.

Bring the long edges together to enclose the cheese and twist. Brush the twists with melted butter, place on the tray and bake for 30 minutes.

toddler task

Brush the melted butter onto the cheese twists prior to baking.

baked pear custard

makes 2 baby portions

olive oil

1 egg

½ cup milk

1 pear, peeled, cored, diced and cooked

nutmeg

Preheat the oven to 180°C and lightly oil a small ramekin. Put the egg and milk into a bowl and beat lightly with a fork. Spoon the pear into the ramekin and pour over the egg mixture. Sprinkle with a little nutmeg and place the ramekin in a larger ovenproof dish. Fill the dish with water until it reaches halfway up the sides of the ramekin. Place on a tray and bake for 40 minutes until the custard has set.

apple and sultana bake

makes 2 baby portions

olive oil

2 apples, peeled, cored and sliced

50 g sultanas

50 g Fruity Bix or Weetbix, crushed

30 g unsalted butter, chopped

Preheat the oven to 180°C and lightly oil a small ovenproof dish. Arrange the apple in the dish. Sprinkle over the sultanas and top with the crushed cereal. Dot with the butter and bake for 20 minutes.

banana crepes

makes 4

olive oil

1 banana

¼ cup coconut milk

4 crepes (see page 64)

Preheat the oven to 160°C and lightly oil a small baking dish. Cut the banana in half and then lengthways, to give 4 pieces. Brush each crepe with coconut milk to soften it, then place a piece of banana in the centre. Carefully roll up, tucking in the edges of the crepe as you do so. Bake for 15 minutes and serve warm.

apricot rice pudding

makes 1 family portion

olive oil

2 eggs

²/₃ cup milk

140 g apricots, cooked and diced

2 cups cooked rice

1 tablespoon caster sugar

Preheat the oven to 180°C and lightly oil a medium-sized oven-proof dish. Whisk the eggs and milk together in a bowl. Stir in the diced apricot, rice and sugar until well combined. Pour into the dish and bake for 30 minutes until lightly golden on top.

peach muffins

makes 24

olive oil

3 cups plain flour

1 tablespoon baking powder

½ cup brown sugar

½ cup caster sugar

140 g peaches, cooked and diced

1 cup milk

125 g unsalted butter, melted

2 eggs, lightly beaten

Preheat the oven to 180°C and lightly oil 2 muffin pans. In a large bowl, sift the flour and the baking powder, then add the remaining ingredients. Stir with a wooden spoon until well combined. Spoon the mixture into the muffin pans and bake for 20–25 minutes. Allow to cool in the pans for 5 minutes, then turn the muffins out onto a wire rack.

toddler task

Sift the flour and baking powder; beat the eggs lightly with a fork.

ONE YEAR PLUS

Some people recommend that a one year old should be eating only 'adult' food, but in reality many parents will still be preparing special food for some time to come. Although there are some foods you will be able to share, it is not realistic to expect your baby to switch automatically to 'adult' food upon turning one. By now your baby has probably progressed to chewy food, but babies develop at different rates and it is important not to push them before they are ready. When they are ready, the following recipes are a good introduction to 'family' or 'adult' food and should prove popular. They are delicious, and of course nutritious, and best of all the whole family can enjoy them, making less work for you!

At the age of one most babies have increased mobility and are learning to walk, hence the term 'toddler'. It is important you do not allow your baby to walk or run around with food as it presents a choking hazard. It is important to encourage the development of good eating habits early.

Your baby's eating patterns may change during this time and

tend towards 'grazing' rather than three meals a day. The amounts they consume will vary day by day. Most babies go through a fussy eating phase, which is a constant source of worry and stress for parents, but try to remember that your baby will eat when they are hungry.

Independence is another trait that will emerge at this age. Babies enjoy finger food as they can manage it well by themselves. Babies are very curious and inquisitive, which leads to them being interested in their food and you may find they are delighted if you take extra care to make it fun.

vegetable frittata

makes 1 family portion

olive oil

1 potato, peeled and finely sliced

1 sweet potato, peeled and finely sliced

1 zucchini

1 red capsicum, seeded and with the veins removed

6 eggs

½ cup milk

½ cup thickened cream

1 cup grated cheddar cheese

2 tablespoons chopped parsley

Preheat the oven to 180°C and lightly oil a 20 cm square baking dish. Steam the potatoes until tender and drain. Cut the zucchini in half and then slice thinly. Cut the capsicum into thin strips. Arrange a layer of potato in the dish, followed by a layer of zucchini and then another of potato. In a large bowl, whisk together the eggs, milk and cream, then stir in the cheese. Pour the mixture over the assembled vegetables and sprinkle with the parsley. Place the dish on a flat baking tray and cook in the oven for 10 minutes. Remove the dish and carefully arrange the capsicum slices on the top, then bake for a further 45 minutes until the egg has set and the top is golden brown. Serve warm or cold.

toddler task

Crack the eggs; stir in the grated cheese; sprinkle the parsley.

pork, celery and apple rolls

makes 10

olive oil

200 g pork fillet, finely sliced

1 stalk celery, peeled and sliced finely

1 apple, peeled, cored and grated

1 litre hot water

10 sheets rice paper

Heat a little oil in a non-stick frypan and add the pork. Cook over a medium heat for 5 minutes, then add the celery and cook for another 5 minutes. Add the apple and reduce the heat to low for 3 minutes.

Pour the hot water into a large shallow dish and soak a sheet of rice paper for 30 seconds. Remove the softened rice paper and place 2 tablespoons of the pork mixture in the centre of the sheet. Carefully fold the sheet over the mixture, then roll it up, tucking in the ends as you go. Repeat with the remaining sheets of rice paper and pork mixture.

toddler task

Count out the rice paper sheets; wash the celery; grate the apple.

beef casserole

makes 4 baby portions

olive oil

1 potato, peeled and diced

1 carrot, peeled and diced

1 zucchini, diced

200 g fillet steak, finely sliced

2 cups salt-reduced beef stock

2 tablespoons tomato paste

¼ cup cornflour

¼ cup water

Preheat the oven to 180°C and lightly oil a small casserole dish with a lid. Steam the potato and carrot until tender, then drain. Place the potato and carrot in the casserole dish with the zucchini and steak. Pour in the beef stock and stir in the tomato paste. Place the dish, covered with its lid, on a flat baking tray and cook in the oven for 1 hour, stirring occasionally. Blend the cornflour and water to form a smooth paste and stir into the casserole. Return to the oven and cook, uncovered, for a further 15 minutes until the sauce has thickened.

toddler task

Wash the zucchini; blend the cornflour and water to a smooth paste.

chicken and basil pasta bake

makes 1 family portion

olive oil

2 spring onions, sliced

1 green capsicum, seeded and diced

6 leaves basil, torn

100 g mushrooms, sliced

1 chicken breast fillet, finely sliced

100 g salt-reduced butter

100 g plain flour

3 cups milk

150 g cheddar cheese, grated

2 litres water

200 g small spiral pasta

Preheat the oven to 180°C and lightly oil a 20 cm baking dish. Heat some oil in a non-stick frypan and sauté the spring onion, capsicum and basil over a medium heat for 5 minutes. Add the mushroom and cook for a further 3 minutes until soft. Transfer to the baking dish. Return the pan to a medium heat, add the chicken and cook for 10 minutes. Add the chicken to the vegetables.

Slowly melt the butter in a large saucepan, then stir in the flour with a wooden spoon. Once combined, cook over a low heat for 2 minutes, stirring constantly. Slowly whisk in the milk to produce a smooth white sauce. Add 50 g of the grated cheese and stir through.

Meanwhile, bring the water to a boil in a large saucepan with a drop of olive oil and add the pasta. Cook for 10 minutes, stirring occasionally, until al dente. Drain the pasta, then combine it with the chicken and vegetables. Pour over the sauce and stir through. Cover the top with the remaining cheese and bake, uncovered, for 30 minutes.

toddler task

Wash the basil and mushrooms; grate the cheese; help to measure the pasta.

*celebrity tip

from Sonia Todd, actor and star of *McLeod's Daughters*

When Sean, my 12-month-old son, is teething he can go off his food a bit, so I do a simple recipe of mashed avocado with cut up fresh prawns and a little pasta or rice – this works 99 per cent of the time.

minestrone

makes 1 family portion

2 tablespoons salt-reduced
   butter

olive oil

1 onion, diced

1 carrot, peeled and diced

1 stalk celery, peeled and diced

100 g green beans, chopped

1 zucchini, diced

1 × 810 g can chopped
   tomatoes

2 tablespoons tomato paste

200 g canned red kidney beans

100 g cooked small pasta

1 litre salt-reduced beef stock

Heat half the butter with a little oil in a large saucepan. Sauté the onion over a medium heat until transparent, about 5 minutes, then add the remaining butter. Stir in the carrot, celery and green beans, then cover and cook for 15 minutes until soft. Add the zucchini and cook for a further 5 minutes. Finally, add the remaining ingredients and simmer, uncovered, for 30 minutes, stirring occasionally.

toddler task
Wash the vegetables; measure the tomato paste.

family meal
Serve minestrone topped with grated parmesan cheese and with a warm crusty breadstick on the side.

lamb and vegetable couscous

makes 1 family portion

olive oil

100 g lamb fillet, finely sliced

100 g pumpkin, peeled and diced

50 g broccoli florets, sliced

1 small carrot, peeled and diced

1¼ cups water

250 g couscous

60 g salt-reduced butter

Heat a little oil in a non-stick frypan and cook the lamb over a medium heat for 5 minutes. Remove and set aside. Add a little more oil to the pan and sauté the vegetables over a medium heat for 15 minutes until soft, then set aside. Boil the water in a large saucepan, then remove from the heat. Gradually add the couscous, stirring constantly for 2 minutes until the liquid has been absorbed. Add the butter and return the pan to a very low heat, then use a fork to separate the grains. Remove from the heat, add the lamb and vegetables and stir well to combine.

stir-fry pork noodles

makes 1 family portion

olive oil

200 g minced pork

1 green capsicum, seeded and diced

100 g bok choy, sliced

50 g dried noodles

1 cup boiling water

¼ cup oyster sauce

Heat a little oil in a non-stick frypan. Place the minced pork in the pan, and break up with a wooden spoon while cooking over a medium heat for 10 minutes. Remove the pork and set aside. Add a little more oil to the pan and sauté the capsicum for 5 minutes until soft. Add the bok choy and cook for a further 3 minutes, then remove from the heat. Soak the noodles in the boiling water for 5 minutes, then loosen with a fork. Drain the noodles and add them to vegetables in the pan. Add the pork and pour in the oyster sauce. Cook over a medium heat for 3 minutes, stirring occasionally.

toddler task

Wash the bok choy; measure the oyster sauce.

chicken and corn parcels

makes 24

olive oil

150 g minced chicken

2 cups water

200 g creamed sweet corn

½ cup grated cheddar cheese

4 sheets puff pastry

50 g salt-reduced butter, melted

Preheat the oven to 180°C and lightly oil a flat baking tray. Place the minced chicken in a medium-sized saucepan with the water. Cover and gently simmer for 15 minutes, occasionally breaking up the mince with a wooden spoon, until the chicken is cooked through. Drain the mince and allow it to cool before combining with the corn and cheese.

Cut each pastry sheet into 6 equal pieces and brush with melted butter. Place a teaspoon of the chicken and corn mixture in the centre of each piece. Carefully lift up the edges of the pastry and seal each parcel by pinching the top together. Brush with melted butter and bake for 30 minutes until golden brown.

toddler task

Use a pastry brush to paint the melted butter onto the pastry.

bolognese sauce

makes 1 family portion

olive oil

1 onion, diced

1 teaspoon dried oregano

2 large mushrooms with the stalks removed, diced

500 g minced steak

1 × 810 g can chopped tomatoes

⅓ cup tomato paste

½ cup water

Heat a little oil in a non-stick frypan and sauté the onion over a medium heat for 5 minutes until transparent. Add the oregano and the mushroom and cook for a further 3 minutes. Add the steak and use a wooden spoon to break up the meat while cooking. Cook for 15 minutes until well browned, then add the tomato. Stir through the tomato paste and water and simmer for 30 minutes, stirring occasionally, until the sauce has reduced and thickened. Serve with your favourite pasta.

family meal

Use this sauce with pasta, gnocchi or to make lasagne.

fresh fish pie

makes 1 family portion

olive oil

200 g John Dory fillet

2 cups water

100 g salt-reduced butter

100 g plain flour

3 cups milk

1 potato, peeled, diced
  and cooked

50 g cooked peas

1 tablespoon chopped parsley

1 sheet puff pastry

20 g salt-reduced butter, melted

Preheat the oven to 180°C and lightly oil a 20 cm square baking dish. Poach the fish by placing it in a large saucepan with the water. Cover and simmer gently for 10 minutes. Remove the fish fillet and flake through with a fork to check there are no bones. Slowly melt the butter in a large saucepan and stir in the flour with a wooden spoon. Once combined, cook over a low heat for 2 minutes, stirring constantly. Slowly whisk in the milk to produce a smooth white sauce. Add the fish, potato, peas and parsley, stirring occasionally while the sauce thickens. Transfer to the baking dish. Lay the pastry on top of the fish mixture and seal the edges. Trim any excess dough and prick the pie a few times with a fork. Brush with melted butter and bake for 30 minutes.

toddler task

Flake through the fish with a fork to check for bones; brush pastry with melted butter.

chicken crepes

makes 4

olive oil

1 zucchini, thinly sliced lengthways

4 chicken tenderloins

4 crepes (see page 63)

50 g salt-reduced butter, melted

Preheat the oven to 160°C and lightly oil a flat baking tray. Heat a little olive oil in a non-stick frypan and sauté the zucchini slices over a medium heat for 5 minutes. Remove from the pan and drain on disposable towel. Cook the chicken in the pan over a medium heat for 10 minutes, browning both sides. Brush each crepe with melted butter to soften it, and place a slice of zucchini and a chicken tenderloin at the centre. Carefully roll up the crepe, place on the baking tray and bake for 10 minutes.

toddler task

Wash the zucchini; brush the crepes with melted butter.

family meal

Place the crepes in a baking dish, pour a cheese sauce (see page 84) over them, and bake at 160°C for 20 minutes until golden. Serve with a green salad.

creamy veal and mushroom pasta

makes 1 family portion

olive oil

200 g veal, finely sliced

50 g mushrooms, diced

50 g plain flour

1 cup salt-reduced beef stock

2 tablespoons tomato paste

⅓ cup thickened cream

1½ litres water

200 g risoni pasta

Heat a little olive oil in a non-stick frypan. Add the veal and cook for 5 minutes over a medium heat. Add the mushrooms and sauté for a further 3 minutes. Reduce the heat to low and add the flour, stirring constantly for 2 minutes. Slowly pour in the stock and stir through the tomato paste. Simmer for 15 minutes, then add the cream and cook for a further 10 minutes until the sauce thickens.

While the sauce is thickening, bring the water to a boil in a large saucepan and add the risoni pasta. Cook for 10 minutes until al dente, stirring occasionally. Drain and serve topped with the veal and mushroom sauce.

quiche lorraine

makes 1 family portion

olive oil	1 cup grated cheddar cheese
2 sheets puff pastry	10 eggs
1 onion, diced	¾ cup milk
4 rashers bacon, diced	½ cup thickened cream
2 tablespoons chopped parsley	

Preheat the oven to 180°C and lightly oil a 22 cm quiche pan. Line the pan using both sheets of pastry and cover with baking paper. Fill the pan with dried cooked rice or weights and 'blind bake' for 20 minutes. Carefully remove the weights or rice and the baking paper and stand the pan on a flat baking tray.

Heat some oil in a non-stick frypan and sauté the onion over a medium heat for 10 minutes until transparent but not coloured. Add the bacon and parsley and cook for a further 5 minutes. Remove from the heat, allow to cool slightly, then scatter over the base of the pastry case.

Sprinkle the cheese on top of the bacon mixture and gently combine. Whisk the eggs, milk and cream in a bowl, then pour into the pastry case. Bake for 30 minutes until the top is lightly golden and the egg has set.

toddler task

Crack the eggs into a cup first to check there is no shell, then transfer to a large mixing bowl.

fish filo parcels

makes 8

olive oil

250 g flake fillets

16 spinach leaves

16 sheets filo pastry

50 g salt-reduced butter, melted

Lightly oil a flat baking tray. Carefully check the fish for any bones and cut the fillets into 10 cm lengths. Remove the stalks from the spinach leaves. Cut the pastry sheets in half and brush with melted butter. Layer four pieces on top of each other. 'Sandwich' the flake between 2 spinach leaves and place at the centre of the pastry. Brush the edges with melted butter, then fold the short ends over and roll to make a parcel, brushing with melted butter to seal the edges. Also brush the top and sides with the melted butter. Repeat with the remaining pastry, spinach and fish, then refrigerate for 30 minutes until the butter is firm. Meanwhile, preheat the oven to 180°C. Put the parcels on the prepared tray and bake for 30 minutes until the pastry is golden brown.

toddler task

Wash the spinach and remove the stalks. Brush the pastry with butter prior to baking.

hearty beef pie

makes 1 family portion

olive oil

250 g fillet steak, finely sliced

100 g sweet potato, peeled and diced

1 small carrot, peeled and diced

50 g mushrooms, diced

130 g salt-reduced butter

½ cup plain flour

2 cups salt-reduced beef stock

1 cup canned crushed tomatoes

1 sheet puff pastry

Preheat the oven to 180°C and lightly oil a 20 cm square casserole dish. Heat a large non-stick frypan and cook the steak over a medium heat for 5 minutes. Remove and set aside. Add some olive oil to the pan and sauté the sweet potato and carrot over a medium heat for 10 minutes until they are soft. Add the mushrooms and cook for a further 3 minutes. Remove from the heat and combine with the steak.

Slowly melt 100 g of the butter in a large saucepan, then stir in the flour with a wooden spoon. Cook over a medium heat, stirring constantly, until the mixture starts to turn golden brown. Slowly whisk in the stock to produce a smooth brown sauce. Reduce the heat and allow to thicken. Add the tomato, steak and vegetables and cook gently for 5 minutes. Transfer the contents to the casserole dish, and top with the pastry. Melt the remaining butter and brush over the pastry. Bake for 30 minutes until the pastry is golden brown.

toddler task
Brush the melted butter over the pastry prior to cooking.

family meal
Serve the pie with creamy mashed potato and zucchini sticks.

---

rice paper rolls
makes 6

1 carrot, peeled

1 zucchini

2 teaspoons salt-reduced butter

6 sheets rice paper

2 cups hot water

Using a potato peeler, shred the carrot into ribbons. Cut the zucchini in half and then lengthways to make thin sticks. Melt the butter in a non-stick frypan, then add the carrot and cook over a medium heat for 5 minutes. Add the zucchini and cook for a further 5 minutes. Remove from the heat and allow to cool. Soak each rice sheet in the hot water for 30 seconds to soften, then drain carefully. Place 1 tablespoon of vegetables in the first third of the rice paper sheet, then roll it firmly, tucking in the edges as you go.

lasagne

makes 1 family portion

100 g mushrooms, stalks removed
olive oil
1 onion, diced
1 teaspoon dried oregano
400 g extra-lean minced steak
1 × 400 g can crushed tomatoes
¼ cup tomato paste
1 cup water

100 g salt-reduced butter
½ cup plain flour
1 teaspoon nutmeg
2 cups milk
1 cup grated cheddar cheese
200 g cooked lasagne sheets
¼ cup grated parmesan cheese

Dice the mushrooms. Heat a little olive oil in a large non-stick frypan. Sauté the onion over a medium heat for 5 minutes until soft but not coloured. Add the mushrooms and oregano and cook for 3 minutes. Add the steak and break up with a wooden spoon during cooking. Cook for 15 minutes until the meat is well browned. Add the tomato, tomato paste and water. Stir well and simmer for 30 minutes, stirring occasionally.

Preheat the oven to 180°C and lightly oil a 20 cm baking dish. Slowly melt the butter in a large saucepan, then stir in the flour with a wooden spoon. Cook over a low heat for 2 minutes, stirring constantly. Add the nutmeg, then slowly whisk in the milk to produce a smooth white sauce. Add half the cheddar cheese and stir for 5 minutes until the sauce has thickened. Remove from the heat.

Place a layer of lasagne sheets in the dish and spoon in half the meat mixture. Cover with half the cheese sauce and repeat the layers. Pour any remaining meat liquid over the lasagne and then cover with the remaining cheddar and the parmesan cheese. Bake for 45 minutes.

chicken and apricot loaf

makes 1 family portion

100 g dried apricots

1 cup warm water

olive oil

500 g minced chicken

50 g spinach, shredded

1 zucchini, grated

½ cup natural yoghurt

¼ cup breadcrumbs

Soak the apricots in the warm water for 30 minutes to soften, then drain and dice. Meanwhile, preheat the oven to 180°C and lightly oil a 30 cm loaf tin. Place the chicken, spinach, zucchini, yoghurt and breadcrumbs in a large bowl and mix well. Add the apricot and spoon the mixture into the loaf tin, pressing down firmly. Bake for 1 hour, then allow to cool slightly and drain any residual juices from the tin. Slice and serve warm.

toddler task
Wash the spinach; grate the zucchini.

beef and lentil balls

makes 16

200 g minced steak

50 g canned brown lentils, washed and drained

1 small carrot, peeled and grated

1 egg, beaten

½ cup breadcrumbs

olive oil

Combine the steak, lentils and carrot in a bowl and mix well. Using your hands, mould the mixture into small balls, dip them into the egg and coat with breadcrumbs. Cook the balls over a medium heat in an oiled non-stick frypan for 15 minutes until golden brown. Drain on disposable towel.

toddler task

Grate the carrot; roll the balls in the breadcrumbs.

chicken and chickpea stir-fry

makes 2 baby portions

1 litre boiling water

30 g dried noodles

100 g chicken breast fillet, finely sliced

olive oil

¼ cup canned chickpeas, washed and drained

¼ cup corn kernels

Pour the boiling water into a large bowl and soak the noodles for 5 minutes, using a fork to break them up. Drain and set aside. Cook the chicken in an oiled non-stick frypan over a medium heat for 5 minutes. Reduce the heat, then add the chickpeas, corn and noodles and cook for a further 5 minutes.

toddler task
Wash and drain the chickpeas.

special fried rice

makes 1 family portion

1 egg

1 tablespoon water

olive oil

3 cups cooked long-grain rice (NB Cook this the day before)

2 rashers bacon, diced and cooked

50 g cooked peas

4 tablespoons soy sauce

Beat the egg and water together lightly with a fork. Pour into a hot, oiled non-stick frypan and cook over a low heat until set. Allow to cool, then roll the egg up, cut it into strips and set aside. Add some oil to the pan and warm the rice over a low heat, stirring constantly with a wooden spoon to break up the grains. Add the egg, bacon and peas and finish off by stirring through the soy sauce.

toddler task

Beat the egg and water together with a fork.

avocado cherry tomatoes

makes about 20

1 avocado, peeled and mashed

2 tablespoons sour cream

1 teaspoon lemon juice

250 g cherry tomatoes

Combine the avocado, sour cream and lemon juice in a bowl. Cover the dip and refrigerate it for 1 hour before using.

Shave a little of the flesh off the base of the tomatoes so they will sit flat on a plate. With a sharp knife cut off the top of each tomato and scoop out the seeds using a teaspoon. Spoon the dip into a piping bag fitted with a star nozzle. Pipe the avocado into the cavity in the cherry tomatoes.

toddler task

Mash the avocado; squeeze the lemon; wash the tomatoes.

mini beef and vegetable pasties

makes 27

olive oil

1 potato, peeled and diced

1 carrot, peeled and diced

100 g pumpkin, peeled and diced

100 g fillet steak, finely sliced

3 sheets puff pastry

50 g salt-reduced butter, melted

Preheat the oven to 180°C and lightly oil a flat baking tray. Heat a little oil in a non-stick frypan, then add the vegetables and cook for 15 minutes until soft. Remove and set aside. Cook the steak in the pan over a high heat for 5 minutes. Add it to the vegetables and allow to cool.

Using a round cutter (or cup) cut 9 rounds from each pastry sheet. Place a teaspoon of mixture in the centre of each round. Fold the edges up and pinch together to make a pastie. Brush with the melted butter and place on the baking tray. Bake for 20 minutes until golden.

toddler task

Brush the pasties with melted butter prior to baking.

family meal

Make bigger pasties using larger pastry rounds and more mixture.

baked ricotta and spinach

makes 2 baby portions

olive oil

1 small handful spinach leaves, stalks removed

¼ cup smooth ricotta cheese

¼ cup grated cheddar cheese

Preheat the oven to 160°C and lightly oil a small baking dish. Layer half the spinach in the dish, then cover with the ricotta cheese and top with the rest of the spinach. Sprinkle with the grated cheese and bake for 20 minutes.

toddler task

Wash the spinach leaves and remove the stalks.

rice cracker sandwich

makes 10

50 g cream cheese, softened

1 teaspoon tomato paste

20 seaweed rice crackers

Combine the cream cheese and tomato paste in a bowl and mix well. Spread the mixture generously onto 10 rice crackers and top each with another cracker to make a 'sandwich'. Allow to stand for 15 minutes to soften, then serve.

broccoli and butter bean bake

makes 2 baby portions

olive oil

1 teaspoon salt-reduced butter

200 g broccoli, chopped

¼ cup canned butter beans, washed and drained

½ cup grated cheddar cheese

Preheat the oven to 180°C and lightly oil a small baking dish. Melt the butter in a non-stick frypan and sauté the broccoli and the butter beans over a medium heat for 5 minutes. Transfer to the baking dish, top with the grated cheese and bake for 10 minutes until the cheese has melted and is golden.

toddler task
Wash and drain the butter beans.

salmon crumpet splits

makes 4

2 crumpet splits cut in half
2 tablespoons cream cheese, softened
50 g smoked salmon, finely sliced

Preheat the griller and toast the crumpets very lightly. Remove
from the heat, then spread generously with the cream cheese and
top with the smoked salmon. Return to the griller for 1 minute until
the salmon is a pale-pink colour. Serve warm.

cheese and tomato tarts

makes 18

olive oil
1 cup grated cheddar cheese
1 cup canned crushed tomatoes
2 sheets puff pastry

Preheat the oven to 180°C and lightly oil 2 muffin pans. Combine
the cheese and tomato in a bowl. Using a round cutter (or cup) cut
9 rounds from each pastry sheet. Gently place the pastry rounds
into the muffin pans using your fingertips to press the pastry into
the moulds. Place enough mixture in each case so that it reaches
only halfway. Bake in the oven for 30 minutes until the pastry is
golden and the cheese has melted.

bacon, zucchini and cheese muffins
makes 24

olive oil

2 cups self-raising flour, sifted

2 rashers bacon, diced and cooked

150 g zucchini, grated

100 g cheddar cheese, grated

60 g salt-reduced butter, melted

1 egg, lightly beaten

1 cup milk

Preheat the oven to 200°C and lightly oil 2 muffin pans. Combine the flour, bacon, zucchini, cheese and butter in a large mixing bowl. Add the egg and milk and stir until just combined. Spoon the mixture into the muffin pans and bake for 20–25 minutes. Cool in the pans for 5 minutes, then transfer to a wire rack.

toddler task
Help to sift the flour; beat the egg.

family meal
Serve with soup (one from this book) for a hearty lunch or easy dinner.

pumpkin loaf

makes 1 family portion

600 g plain flour

¼ cup full-cream milk powder

1 teaspoon salt

30 g butter, softened

3 teaspoons dry yeast

1 cup warm water

200 g pureed pumpkin

olive oil

1 egg yolk, beaten

Sift the flour, milk powder and salt into a large bowl and rub in the butter using your fingertips. Dissolve the yeast in half the warm water. Make a well in the centre of the dry ingredients, then add the yeast mixture and pureed pumpkin. Mix to form a dough, adding extra water as required. Turn the dough onto a floured board and knead until smooth. Place in a lightly oiled bowl, then cover and allow to stand in a warm place for 30 minutes until the dough has doubled in bulk. Turn the dough out onto a floured board, then knock it down. Meanwhile, preheat the oven to 200°C and lightly oil a 30 cm loaf tin. Knead the dough for a few minutes and put it in the loaf tin. Allow to stand in a warm place for 30 minutes.

Brush the top of the loaf with egg yolk and bake for 15 minutes. Reduce the heat to 180°C and bake for a further 20 minutes. Allow to stand in the tin for 5 minutes, then transfer to a wire rack.

avocado and cheese muffins

makes 2 baby portions

½ avocado

1 teaspoon lemon juice

2 English muffins

½ cup grated cheddar cheese

Mash the avocado and stir in the lemon juice. Split the muffins and lightly toast the base under the griller. Spread the other side with a layer of avocado and sprinkle generously with the cheese. Grill until the cheese is bubbling and golden. Cut each muffin in half and serve warm.

tomato, cheese and basil rounds

makes 6

olive oil

6 slices toast bread

1 large tomato, washed and sliced

6 basil leaves, washed

¼ cup grated cheddar cheese

Preheat the oven to 180°C and lightly oil a flat baking tray. Using a fluted scone cutter, cut a round from each bread slice. Top with a slice of tomato and a basil leaf, then sprinkle with grated cheese. Bake in the oven for 15 minutes until the cheese is golden.

strawberry and rhubarb mousse

makes 6

olive oil

250 g strawberries, hulled and chopped

100 g rhubarb, peeled and chopped

½ cup caster sugar

1½ cups water

½ cup natural yoghurt

10 g gelatine

¼ cup boiling water

Lightly oil 6 individual moulds or a 1-litre capacity dish. Place the strawberry, rhubarb and half the caster sugar in a saucepan with the water. Cover and cook over a low heat for 15 minutes. Drain off the liquid and allow the fruit to cool, then blend to a puree. Stir through the yoghurt and remaining sugar. In a separate bowl, sprinkle the gelatine onto the boiling water and stir thoroughly to ensure it dissolves completely. Slowly whisk the yoghurt mixture into the dissolved gelatine until combined. Pour into the moulds and refrigerate overnight.

toddler task

Wash the strawberries and the rhubarb.

baked peaches with mascarpone cheese

makes 1 baby portion

olive oil

1 peach

1 teaspoon honey

1 tablespoon mascarpone cheese

Preheat the oven to 160°C and lightly oil a shallow ovenproof dish. Cut the peach in half and carefully remove the stone with a teaspoon. Shave a small piece of flesh off each half so they will sit flat in the dish, flesh-side up. Drizzle the honey over the top and bake for 30 minutes. Allow to cool slightly, then dice and combine with the mascarpone cheese.

family meal

Serve the peach halves with mascarpone cheese in the cavity, garnished with fresh mint.

bread, butter and date pudding

makes 1 family portion

olive oil

50 g dates

½ cup warm water

2 slices day-old bread

20 g salt-reduced butter

2 eggs

¼ cup caster sugar

1 cup milk

1 cup thickened cream

Preheat the oven to 180°C and lightly oil a small, shallow oven-proof dish. Soak the dates in the warm water for 15 minutes, then drain and slice finely. Remove the crusts from the bread, butter each slice and cut into triangles. Arrange the bread in the dish and sprinkle the dates over the bread. In a large bowl, whisk together the eggs and sugar and add the milk and cream. Pour the milk mixture over the bread. Place the dish in a larger one and stand both on a flat baking tray. Fill the larger dish with enough hot water to reach halfway up the side of the smaller one. Bake for 40 minutes until the egg mixture has set and the top of the pudding is golden.

toddler task

Crack the eggs; sprinkle the dates over the bread.

rhubarb and cream cheese tartlets

makes 18

100 g rhubarb, trimmed and chopped

1 cup water

¼ cup caster sugar

250 g cream cheese, softened

2 sheets sweet shortcrust pastry

Preheat the oven to 180°C and lightly oil 2 muffin pans. Place the rhubarb in a saucepan with the water, then cover and cook over a low heat for 10 minutes. Add the sugar and cook, uncovered, for a further 5 minutes, stirring constantly. Allow to cool, then drain off half the liquid and blend until smooth. Whisk in the cream cheese. Using a round cutter (or cup) cut 9 rounds from each pastry sheet. Gently place the pastry rounds into the muffin pans, using your fingertips to press the pastry into the moulds. Fill with the cream cheese mixture and bake for 30 minutes.

summer berry pudding

makes 1 family portion

¾ cup water

10 g gelatine

500 g strawberries, hulled and sliced

8 slices white bread

Bring the water to a boil in a saucepan. Sprinkle in the gelatine and stir thoroughly to ensure it dissolves completely. Reduce the heat, then add the strawberries and cook for 10 minutes, stirring occasionally. Allow to cool slightly. Remove the crusts from the bread and line a small bowl with the bread, cutting it to fit snugly. Spoon in the strawberries, reserving the liquid. Top with another layer of bread and pour over the remaining liquid. Weight down with pastry weights or a heavy dish, then cover and refrigerate overnight.

toddler task

Wash the strawberries.

fruit scones

makes 12

olive oil

2 cups plain flour

1 teaspoon baking powder

½ teaspoon salt

50 g unsalted butter, softened

¾ cup milk

¼ cup mixed dried fruit, glace cherries removed

Preheat the oven to 200°C and lightly oil a flat baking tray. Sift the flour and baking powder into a large mixing bowl. Add the salt and butter and rub together with fingers until combined. Make a well in the centre, then add most of the milk and mix with a knife to form a dough. Add the fruit and turn the dough out onto a floured board. Knead and flatten to a thickness of approximately 2 cm. Cut rounds with a scone cutter and place on the tray. Brush the tops with the remaining milk and bake for 15 minutes. Transfer to a wire rack to cool.

toddler task

Remove the glace cherries from the dried fruit; help to sift the flour and baking powder.

mini apple tarts

makes 6

olive oil

1 sheet shortcrust pastry

2 Granny Smith apples, peeled, cored and finely sliced

3 tablespoons caster sugar

30 g unsalted butter

1 egg

1 tablespoon milk

Preheat the oven to 200°C and lightly oil a flat baking tray. Cut the pastry sheet into 6 equal pieces. Layer the slices of apple over each piece leaving a 1-cm border. Carefully turn up the border to form a 'lip', pinching the corners to seal. Sprinkle with some sugar and dot with butter. Whisk the egg and milk together in a small bowl and brush the sides of each tart. Place on the tray and bake for 15 minutes.

toddler task

Crack the egg; sprinkle the sugar over the tarts.

baby muesli biscuits

makes 40

½ cup dried apples

1 cup warm water

olive oil

200 g unsalted butter, softened

½ cup brown sugar

1 egg

2 cups baby muesli with oat flakes and apple

1 cup self-raising flour

½ cup sultanas

Soak the dried apples in the warm water for 30 minutes and, when soft, drain and dice them. Preheat the oven to 180°C and lightly oil a flat baking tray. Using an electric beater, cream the butter and sugar together for 5 minutes until pale yellow. Add the egg and beat until combined. Stir in the apple, muesli, flour and sultanas and mix well. Using a teaspoon, drop balls of the mixture onto the baking tray and flatten with wet fingertips. Leave sufficient room between the biscuits for them to spread during cooking. Bake for 15 minutes until brown. Allow to cool on the tray.

toddler task

Crack the egg; measure out the apples and sultanas.

apple and pear crumble

makes 1 family portion

olive oil

2 Granny Smith apples, peeled, cored and sliced

2 pears, peeled, cored and sliced

½ cup plain flour

1 cup one-minute oats

2 tablespoons caster sugar

80 g unsalted butter, softened

Preheat the oven to 180°C and lightly oil a medium-sized oven-proof dish. Place a layer of apple in the dish, then a layer of pear. Combine the flour, oats, sugar and butter in a food processor. Spoon over the fruit, pat down and bake for 30 minutes until golden.

toddler task

Layer the apple and pear in the baking dish.

strawberry yoghurt icy poles

makes 4

125 g strawberries, hulled and diced

¾ cup natural yoghurt

Combine the strawberries and yoghurt in a bowl. Spoon into plastic icy-pole moulds, insert the sticks and place in the freezer to set. To remove the icy poles, place the moulds under hot running water briefly.

toddler task

Wash the strawberries and help to mix with the yoghurt.

*celebrity tip

from Jim Wilson, television sports presenter

The thing with Joe is that I want him to eat anything that is put in front of him, and the more savoury foods he can handle the better. Jackie and I hate sweets and Joseph will have little choice but to like 'grazing' and sampling as many tastes as possible. That's the great thing about this country – the Italians, Greeks, Lebanese and Vietnamese have given us so much to choose from. Good eating, keep it simple, fresh is best – enjoy the delights of food. Joe certainly will!

INDEX